D0231745

Aberdeenshire Library and Information Service
www.aberdeenshire.gov.uk/libraries
Renewals Hotline 01224 661511

1 0 DEC 2008
15. 12. DEC
29. DEC 08.
05. MAY 09.

18. OCT 13.

1 4 OCT 2017

22. AUG 14.

2 1 APR 2018

10. 06. 15.

2 2 JUN 2009

1 6 JUL 2015

− 4 MAY 2018

− 3 APR 2019

12. AUG 10.

05. APR 11.
02. FEB 12.

− 5 AUG 2015

2 8 NOV 2015

28 JUN 19.

28. MAY 13.

2 8 JUL 2016

30. OCT 19.

1 0 JUL 2017

28. FEB 14

−1 AUG 2017

Wentworth, Patri

The girl in the
cellar /
Patricia

LP

1828435

THE GIRL IN THE CELLAR

THE GIRL
IN THE CELLAR

PATRICIA WENTWORTH

LARGE PRINT
Oxford

First published in Great Britain 1961
by
Hodder & Stoughton

Published in Large Print 2008 by ISIS Publishing Ltd.,
7 Centremead, Osney Mead, Oxford OX2 0ES
by arrangement with
Hodder & Stoughton Ltd.,
a division of HLUK (Euston Road) Ltd.

British Library Cataloguing in Publication Data
Wentworth, Patricia
    The girl in the cellar. – Large print ed.
    1. Silver, Maud (Fictitious character) – Fiction
    2. Detective and mystery stories
    3. Large type books
    I. Title
    823.9'12 [F]

ISBN 978–0–7531–8126
ISBN 978–0–7531–8127–0 (pb)

Printed and bound in Great Britain by
T. J. International Ltd., Padstow, Cornwall

The tale is mine, the punctuation yours.
Oh, happy envied fate that this affords,
Firmly to dam with strong and silent stops
The flowing torrent of a woman's words!

CHAPTER
ONE

She looked into the dead unbroken dark and had neither memory nor thought. She was not conscious of where she was, or of how she had come there. She was not conscious of anything except the darkness. She did not know if time had passed. There seemed to be no sense that it went by, but it must have done, because the moment when she knew nothing except the darkness had changed into a moment in which she knew that her feet were on stone, and that she must not move from where she stood.

A gradual knowledge invaded her, and with it a fear that was like the beginning of pain. She did not know how the knowledge came to her. She only knew that it was there. The stone under her feet was a step. It was a single step in a long stone flight. If she were to move she might fall, she did not know how far. The thought terrified her. It came to her, she did not know how, that it was not the unknown depth that was the terror behind her thought, but the thing that waited there. Her heart knocked and her knees shook. Whatever happened, she must not fall. Every instinct told her that. She felt behind her and found a step above the one upon which she stood. The darkness round her had begun to break into fiery sparks as she sank down and leaned forward with her head between her knees. Afterwards she was to think how strange it was that she should remember the right thing to do if you thought you were going to faint.

Presently the fiery sparks died out and the darkness was quite dark again. She put down her hand and felt the step on which she was sitting. It was cold and damp — and it was stone, just as she had known that it would be. Moving along it her hand touched something else. The warmer, drier feel of leather or plastic came to her. The thing moved with the movement of her hand. It was a handbag. She drew it towards her, set it in her lap, and felt for the clasp. It had an unfamiliar feeling. You ought to know how to open your own bag, but it felt strange — her fingers fumbled with it.

And then all at once the clasp moved and the bag was open. She slipped her hand inside it and felt the smooth, cool shape of the pocket-torch — felt it and let go of it again.

Of course she must have dropped her bag when she came down the steps. She had come down the steps with her bag, and she had dropped it. Why had she come down the steps? She didn't know, any more than she knew who she was, or where this place might be. There was only one thing she did know, and that was that someone was lying dead at the bottom of the steps.

She didn't know how she knew it, but she did know it, just as she knew with a sharp and terrible conviction that she must get away quickly, quickly, whilst she could. She got to her feet, when something halted the panic impulse. It was like a voice speaking in her mind. It said quite definitely, clearly, and soberly, "You can't just run away and not see whether there is anything you can do."

She remembered the torch, and was afraid. There was a dead girl lying at the foot of these stone steps. She knew it with the same ultimate certainty with which she knew that she was there herself, and she knew that she couldn't just go away and leave her without looking with her eyes to back up that certainty. She took the torch out of the bag and switched it on. The small wavering beam cut the darkness and showed her what she had known she would see. She had known it because she had seen it before. She had stood as she was standing now, but the beam had been brighter then. It had come from a larger torch. She looked along this narrower, feebler beam and saw the girl lie there where she had pitched forward at the foot of the steps. She had been going down them, and she had been shot from behind. She lay with her hands stretched out and a dreadful wound in her head.

The girl on the steps went down the last six. She went round the body, keeping the light away from the head. She bent down and took hold of one of those outflung wrists. It was cold, and it was beginning to be stiff. There was no pulse. She straightened up and turned with the torch in her hand.

The place was a cellar, quite bare, quite empty. The light picked up splinters of glass. There was a broken torch that lay against the right side of the dead girl's body. It came to her that it was the stronger torch which she had used on the other side of the black wall past which she could not go. She had used it, and she had dropped it, and it had rolled and come to rest beside the poor broken girl at the foot of the steps.

She turned now and went to the steps. There was nothing she could do, no help or comfort she could give. She must get away. She went up two steps, and then fear came on her. The lighted torch was in her hand. She switched it off and waited for her heart to stop knocking against her side. It took a long time to steady down. When at last it was going at a slower and more even pace, she opened her eyes again and saw very dimly the rising steps that were there in front of her and the shape of the doorway through which she must have come, a dimly lighted shape high up in a wall of darkness.

She began to walk up the steps towards the open door. She was conscious of two things only. They were on different levels of consciousness. One of them was the torch. It was in the bag again — she must have put it there. Her consciousness would not let go of it. She could feel the shape of it still in her hand, but it wasn't there any longer. The bag was there. The other thing was on a different plane. She must get away. That was the flooding necessity. It struck her like one of those big waves which hit you when you are bathing in the sea and knock you down and break over you. When she looked back she could not really remember how she got out of the house, only that it wasn't quite dark in the hall, and that the door — the front door — wasn't latched. Her full consciousness, her memory, came back to the moment when she found herself standing at the end of the road and looking at the traffic that went by.

CHAPTER
TWO

She sat in the bus. It was full of people, but she did not really see them. They were there, but she felt herself separate from them — apart. It was as if she was in one story and they in another, as if the stories had nothing to do with one another, as if there was something like a sheet of glass between them and her, between her consciousness and theirs, and no communication was possible.

There was money in her purse. When the conductor came round she took out a two-shilling bit and paid her fare. The curious thing was that when she was getting the money out she had no idea how much to give, and then quite suddenly she did know, so that what had begun as a vague adventure slipped over into a mechanical action too accustomed to need conscious thought.

When the bus stopped at the station she got out and looked about her. There ought to be luggage. She was going on a journey, and you don't do that without luggage. It puzzled her, because just for a moment she could see her luggage — a trunk and a hat-box. She could see them quite clearly, but when she tried to see the name on them the whole thing went. She shut her eyes for a moment against the dizziness which followed. When she opened them it was all gone. She wasn't sure about anything any more.

Someone touched her on the arm. A very kind voice said, "Are you all right?"

She turned and looked round on the little lady who was exactly like the governesses you read about in Victorian and early Edwardian books, quite out of date and tremendously reassuring. No one who looked like that could have any connection with a dark, secret, underground crime. She found herself smiling. She heard herself say, "Oh, yes, I'm all right, thank you."

She did not, of course, know that her smile was the most heartbreaking thing in the world, any more than she knew that there was no colour at all in her face.

Miss Silver looked at her with concern. It was not in her to go on her way and leave a fellow creature to chance. The girl looked as if she might faint at any moment. She had the unrecollected air of one who has had a terrible shock, and who has not yet come to terms with it. She put out a hand and touched the girl's arm again.

"Will you have a cup of tea with me, my dear?"

The pale lips moved. She said, "Thank you," with something heartfelt in her tone. The hand that had touched her was slipped inside her arm. There was one more look round for the luggage that wasn't there, and then with a most curious feeling of relief she was going through the arch with Miss Silver. They came into a cross-stream of traffic which made her feel shaken and giddy. Then in a vague unthinking way she was turning to her companion, and this vague and instinctive movement was at once met with a most practical and efficient kindness. Her cold ungloved hand was taken. She felt the presence of a sustaining kindness, and for the moment needed nothing more. She was aware of guidance. Her eyes dropped from the rush and hurry of the crowd they were passing through. And then all at once a glass-topped door was opened and shut again, the noise of the hurry and rush was left outside. It was as if she had passed into another state of being, one in which there was kindness and protection, she did not know from what. She only knew that it was warm, and that she was safe. She sat down with her back to the wall, and there was an interval. Then the little lady's voice again, "Drink your tea, my dear, while it is hot."

She opened her eyes. There was a cup of tea, and as soon as she saw it she knew that she was faint from long abstinence. She put out her hand to the cup, lifted it, and drank. The tea was very milky. She drained the cup and set it down, her eyes open now and seeing. They saw the crowded room and the little lady sitting opposite to her and pouring out tea. She had small, neat features and the sort of old-fashioned clothes that were not so much dowdy as characteristic. She had on a black coat and a black hat with a trail of red roses on one side and a row of little black poofs of net on the other. The little black poofs began quite big at the back of the hat and got smaller all the way until they reached the front, where they met the last red bud of the trail of roses.

8

Miss Silver smiled and filled her cup. When she had done this without hurry she lifted a plate of cakes and held them out. The girl looked at them, looked at Miss Silver, put out a hand, came near to touching a cake, and paused there, her eyes fixed on Miss Silver's face. She heard her voice say, "I don't know — what money — I have —"

The little lady straightened herself. She smiled.

"You are having tea with me, my dear."

She took the nearest bun. She knew an animal hunger. She wanted to cram it into her mouth. She took the bun and lifted it slowly to her lips. Her hand shook. The worst was when the food was at her lips. She had to take a moment then to control the dreadful animal impulse. When she had mastered it she took the food and ate it slowly, delicately. A feeling of confidence came to her. She ate the rest of the bun, and she drank about half the tea.

The little lady's hand offered the plate again. This time it was not such a struggle.

When she had eaten three buns and had two cups of the warm milky tea she felt better. It crossed her mind then to wonder when she had eaten last. She couldn't remember — she couldn't remember at all.

She stopped trying to remember. It wasn't any good. When she looked back it was like looking into a thick blinding fog. She couldn't see anything at all. She couldn't see past the moment when she stood on the cellar steps in the dark and strained her eyes. A shudder went over her, and with the shudder she moved.

Miss Silver said in a quiet, kind voice, "What is it, my dear?"

She could hear the beginnings of panic in her own voice as she said, "I don't know —"

"Your name — is that it?"

She gave a little frightened nod.

"I don't know — who I am —"

"Have you looked in your bag?" Miss Silver's eyes were on her, kind and steady.

"No. I took some money out for the bus —"

"Yes, I saw you do that."

"I took it out, but — I can't remember —"

"Suppose you look and see."

"Yes, I could do that, couldn't I?"

She put a hand on the bag to open it and then stopped, she could not have said why. Afterwards when she looked back she remembered that moment — her hand on the bag ready to open it, and something that stopped her. It was there, and then it was gone again and she didn't know why it had come. Her hand resumed its interrupted motion and the bag was opened.

She looked down into it. It was a black bag with a grey lining. It didn't feel as if it was hers. It was a new bag. There was a handkerchief in it, and a mirror. She thought that she had seen them before. And then, quickly on that, "Oh, but I have — I must have — because I paid the fare on the bus." The thought came and was gone again. The bag had a middle partition. She opened it and looked down at the money. On one side there were a lot of notes. On the other side there was change. She heard herself say in a dazed sort of voice, "I've got quite a lot of money — quite a lot —"

Miss Silver said, "That is all to the good, my dear."

She lifted the pathetic grey eyes and said, "But I didn't open this — I'm sure I didn't —"

Miss Silver's voice came to her.

"Try the other side of the bag."

There was a little grey pocket high up on the side. She remembered opening it in the bus. She opened it now, and remembered that she had opened it before — in the bus, when the conductor came round to take the fares. She had given him a two-shilling bit, and that had left a little loose pile of silver and coppers. Her fare had been fourpence, and she had put the change back, twopence and a sixpence and a shilling, and had fastened the purse again.

She said, "Yes, it was here," and felt an unreasoned, unreasoning sense of relief. And then on that a clouding, because she didn't know really what she was looking for, or why she had been looking for it.

She drew a long breath and took one hand from the bag and lifted it to her face. She didn't know. There was a moment when everything ran together in her mind — when all the moments were one moment. It was rather dizzying and frightening. She leaned her head on her hand and it passed. When she looked up again the moment of confusion was gone.

She said, "What was I doing?"

And Miss Silver said in her kind firm voice, "There is a letter in your bag. Suppose you look at it."

"Yes — yes, I will."

She tilted the bag and saw the letter. She took it out, looking at the wrong side of the envelope first and then turning it over. It was addressed to Mrs James Fancourt.

Was that her name? She didn't know.

A feeling of sharp terror passed over her so quickly that she scarcely knew it for what it was. The bag sank down upon the table and left her with the letter in her hand.

Miss Silver was watching her closely, but she was aware of nothing but the letter.

Mrs James Fancourt . . . the name was utterly strange to her, and because it was so strange her fingers stopped in what they were doing. You can't open someone else's letter. And then, quick on that, the memory of a dead girl in a cellar. "It's hers, or it's mine. If it's hers, she's gone. Someone must read it. If it's mine, I must read it." The thoughts ran through her head quickly, so very quickly. Her hand took up the letter.

It was open. She took it out of the envelope, unfolded it, and read:

Chantreys,
Haleycott.

Dear Anne,

It is very difficult to know how to write, but we have Jim's letter and we will do what he asks us to and take you in. It is all very worrying. Jim's letter is very short and does not really tell us anything, only that he has married you, and that you will be

12

arriving. It all seems very strange. But of course we
will do what we can. I don't at all understand why
he has not come over with you.

Yours affectly.
Lilian Fancourt.

She looked up, met Miss Silver's eyes, and at once
looked down again. When she had read the letter a
second time she held it out, her gaze wide and fixed.

"I don't know what it means."

Miss Silver took the letter and read it through. Then
she held out her hand for the envelope. It was
addressed to Mrs James Fancourt, just that and nothing
more. A personal letter sent by hand. By whose hand?
There was no answer to the question.

Miss Silver said, "How did this reach you?"

"I don't know —"

"Do not trouble yourself. Are there any other letters
in your bag?"

"I don't think so —"

"Will you look?"

She looked, but there was nothing more — nothing
but that one link with the past, with the future.

Miss Silver said, "Why did you come to this station?"

The dark blue eyes looked through a mist of tears.

"I don't know — I don't seem to know anything —"

It was clear to Miss Silver that she was at the end of
her resources. Nothing would be gained by continuing
to press for an answer which was not there. She said
very kindly, "Do not trouble yourself, my dear. It is
very fortunate that you have this address and the

13

assurance that these relatives of your husband are awaiting your arrival affectionately. As to who they are, you will know more when you have met them. This place is not so very far away."

"You know it?"

"I have never been there, but a friend of mine was staying in the neighbourhood recently."

The words seemed to bring the unknown Haleycott a little nearer. Anne . . . that felt right. Anne . . . her mother called her that a long time ago. She said, "You think I ought to go there?"

Miss Silver's voice was very kind as she answered.

"Yes, I think so. You are expected, and if you do not come there will be anxiety. I do not think you ought to trouble yourself too much. Memory is a curious thing. You may wake up tomorrow and find that everything is clear again."

CHAPTER
THREE

She could never remember much about that journey. When she thought about it afterwards it resolved itself into something like a dream. There was the swaying of the train and the warmth of the carriage. Those two things she remembered, but nothing more. She thought that she slept a little, and woke again in a panic of fear lest she should have passed her station. And after that she stayed awake, but nothing felt real except the rushing of the train and the darkness close up against the windows. It was as if she was in a closed-in space and she was safe as long as she was there. Only she mustn't rely upon this safety and fall asleep again.

The other people in the carriage came and went. The train stopped a good deal. Haleycott was a little place. Anything that stopped there would stop at a great many other places too. There was an elderly woman who looked at her very hard, and a young one, gay and laughing with a boy of her own age. They got out, and two other people got in, a woman and a child of about six.

And then they were at Haleycott. Anne got to her feet. She looked about her for her hat-box.

There wasn't any hat-box.

And then she got out on to the platform and stood there with the most terribly lost feeling she had ever had. The train she had left was leaving her. She was a stranger in a strange place. A feeling of utter desolation swept over her, and then, hard upon it, something stronger. It was like the sun coming out. There, on the dim platform with the darkness crowding in, the light began to shine inside her. She stopped being afraid. She stopped thinking of all the things that might be going to happen. Her shoulders straightened up. She began to walk along the little station platform as if she had known it all her life, as if she was coming home.

There was a cab and she got into it. She said no, there was no luggage, and she gave the address that was on the letter in her bag. And then they were off.

She didn't know what she thought of whilst they were driving. She didn't know whether she thought of anything at all. When she thought about it afterwards there was only that feeling of a rising sun. There were good things that were going to happen in the coming day. It was a strange thing, but it did not seem strange to her, it felt perfectly natural.

The wheels went round, and presently the wheels stopped. She got out, paid the man, and pulled the old-fashioned bell. It was not quite dark here. She could see the shape of the door and the line of the house with the small yellow lamps of the waiting taxi.

And then the hall door moved. At once she stepped forward. It was as if the opening of the door was like the rising of the curtain in a theatre, a signal for the play to begin. A woman stood there. She wore a brown

16

dress and an apron. She had a quantity of grey hair. She said, "Oh, Mrs Jim!" And then she turned and called over her shoulder, "Oh, Miss Lilian, it's Mrs Jim!" Then, with a quick turn back to the door, she put out both her hands and said in a warm, full voice, "Oh, my dear — what a coming home to be sure! But come you in — come you in!"

The taxi rolled away behind her and was gone. She walked into the hall of the house and saw Lilian Fancourt coming down the stair at the far end of it.

She knew who it was. That was one of the things that you think about afterwards. At the time there was no place for thought. Things kept happening.

Lilian Fancourt came down the stair with her hands out in welcome. Everything about her said the word. Everything about her said what wasn't true. She came forward, she reached up, put her little hands on the tall girl's shoulders and kissed her, and it was all like a scene from a play. There was no reality in it.

CHAPTER
FOUR

"Of course, I don't know how much you know."

If Miss Fancourt had said that once, she had said it so many times that one's mind stopped being able to take it in, and then each time she had leaned across to press her hand and to say, "Oh, but we mustn't. We mustn't dwell on all that, must we?"

The first two or three times it happened Anne found herself saying "No." And then it came home to her, that it wasn't a thing to be answered — it was just her way of talking, so she didn't say anything at all.

The woman who had let her in, and whose name was quite unbelievably Thomasina Twisledon, took her upstairs and along a wide passage to her room. She thought it would look out on the back, and was vaguely pleased, she didn't know why. There was a bathroom next door, and Thomasina said the water was always hot.

Anne found herself taking off her hat and her coat and looking into the glass to see whether her hair was tidy. She didn't know what she expected to see when she looked in the glass. Everything was so strange. Would what she saw be strange too — another Anne whom she had never seen before, looking at her from a dream life which had no connection with reality?

She looked into the mirror and saw herself — her own real self. The relief was so great that the face she looked at, with its brown curling hair, its dark blue eyes, its parted lips, swam in a sudden mist. She leaned on her hands and let the giddiness go by.

Thomasina stood on the other side of the bed and watched her. In her own mind she was saying things like "Oh, my poor dear, you don't know what you've come to! And there's nothing I can do — there's nothing anyone can do!"

The moment passed. Anne straightened up and turned. She went into the bathroom and washed, and then she went downstairs with Thomasina and into the little sitting-room on the left-hand side of the hall.

Lilian Fancourt was sitting there knitting. She began almost before Anne was in the room.

"Are you very tired? Oh, you must be, I'm sure! Thomasina will bring you something to eat, and then you must get to bed! Oh, yes, I must insist upon that! Now, Thomasina, what shall it be? We mustn't let her think that we mean to starve her here. What do you think?"

"I'll see what cook's got ready," said Thomasina, and was gone.

Lilian Fancourt put her knitting down on her knee.

"You'd think she'd be more interested," she said in a light complaining tone. "She's been with us thirty years. It just shows, doesn't it?" She picked up her knitting again. "Do you like this? It was meant to be a

19

jumper for me, but of course I don't know whether I shall wear it now."

Thomasina went through to the kitchen. It was not the old kitchen of the house — that had been abandoned sixty or seventy years ago. She went through a door at the back of the hall and along a stone passage until she came to it. There was a little elderly woman there with light frizzy blonde hair done up in a bun. She wore a dark grey dress with a big cook's apron covering it so that only the sleeves and a bit of the hem showed. She was sitting at the kitchen table with a pack of cards spread out before her. She said without looking up, "Well, has she come?"

Thomasina said heavily, "Ay, she's come, Mattie. I'm to take along a tray."

Mattie gave a little crow.

"And what did I tell you, Thomasina! P'raps you'll believe me another time! She'll come here and she'll eat and drink solitary — that's what I said not later than yesterday! But you didn't believe me, now did you?"

Thomasina said, "No, I didn't believe you, nor I won't never, and not a bit of good your going on about it, Mattie. She looks as if what she needs most is a week in bed, the poor child!"

Mattie Oliver threw her a quick darting glance and chuckled.

"Oh, that's the way of it, is it? Haven't you never had enough of putting people on pedestals and seeing them come topplin' down? Oh, all right, all right, I'm a'comin', aren't I?"

On the other side of the house Anne felt the time go by fitfully, crazily. Lilian Fancourt never stopped talking, and it was all about nothing at all. There was no end to it. Your mind shut off in the middle of how inconvenient it was to have only two maids where there used to be seven or eight, and you came back to a long plaintive wail about how times had changed since the war.

"But what I say is, there's no need to change because other people do. My father never changed, never in the least, down to the day of his death a couple of years ago. He was ninety-five, you know, and he used to go out shooting until that last winter. Jim always said, 'Let him alone — let him do what he wants to.' In fact I don't know who was going to stop him. Not poor little me!" She looked up coyly as she spoke.

Jim — Anne's mind closed against the name. Not now — not here — not until she was fed and rested.

But Lilian Fancourt went on talking about him. Jim said this, and Jim said that, and Jim said the other.

And then the door opened and Thomasina came in with the tray. It was a blessed relief, because Lilian stopped talking about Jim. She looked up suddenly and said, "Where is Harriet?"

Thomasina said, "She's not in yet."

Lilian made a little vexed sound.

"Oh dear — Father wouldn't have liked it at all — not at all!"

And on that Harriet came in.

She was so tall that she seemed to look down upon Anne. She was so tall that she seemed to look down on herself. She had a small head on the top of a tall, lanky body, and she wore the kind of dark clothes that look as if they are meant to be mourning. Her hat was pushed back on her head. A capacious but shabby bag swung from her left hand. She put out the right with a curious poking effect, looked past Anne, and said with an odd rush of words, "I'm so sorry. Not to be in when you came. Have you been here long?"

CHAPTER
FIVE

When she tried to remember the rest of the evening she couldn't. It was just a wash of pale-tinted platitudes. She was aware of Lilian, who talked incessantly and never said anything that you could remember, and of Harriet, who sat in the sofa corner with her eyes on what looked like a parish magazine. Every now and then she said something of what she was reading — "Mr Wimbush says —" or, "Miss Brown writes —"

Thomasina came in to take the tray. Going out with it, she turned and surveyed the scene.

"If you were to ask me, I'd say early to bed — that's what I'd say."

The words came into the fog in which Anne was. They seemed to start in her brain, in her heart, and to flow out from there until the room was full of them. For the last half-hour Lilian Fancourt's words had come and gone in the fog, come and gone again. She lifted her eyes and looked across to where Thomasina stood by the door. She couldn't see her distinctly because of the mist in the room. She didn't know that her eyes looked through the fog with a desperate appeal.

Thomasina went out of the room, and she had a moment of absolute desolation. And then in what felt like the same moment she was back again. The door hadn't shut. It couldn't have shut, because it didn't open again. Thomasina was there one moment, and the next she was coming back. She came back into the room and across it.

"You're coming to bed, Mrs Jim!" she said. "If ever I see anyone ready for bed, it's you, my poor dear, so you'll just come along!"

Anne got up on her feet with a steadying arm to hold her. She said good-night to Lilian, and goodnight to Harriet, and she got out of the room. She didn't know what they said in reply.

Lilian had a good deal to say. The words drifted lightly by and were gone. Harriet detached herself momentarily from the parish magazine. She said in a surprised voice, "Oh, are you going? Good-night." And then Thomasina had her through the door and it was shut.

She was in that state where the ordinary restraints are gone. She did not know that she was going to speak, but she heard herself saying, "I don't belong anywhere — I just don't belong." And then there was a kind of blank. They were going up the stairs. It was very difficult. She did her best, but it was very difficult. She was aware of Thomasina's arm at her waist and of the baluster rail under her hand. The stairs took a long time to climb — a long, long time. There were times when she didn't know what she was doing — times when Thomasina's encouraging voice went away to the

24

merest whisper, so faint that she could not really hear it. There were times when she didn't know anything at all. And yet all these times passed. There came the moment when she felt the pillow under her head, and the moment when the light went out and left her free to a world of sleep.

Time passed — a lot of time. She roused up once and stirred in bed, to feel an exquisite relief and sink again into that deep, deep sleep.

When at last she awoke it was light outside. She lay for a few moments seeing the strange room but not fully conscious of it. There was sunshine outside the window and a twittering of birds — sunshine and bird song. She drew in a long breath and began to remember.

The day before. It was like unpacking a crowded, ill-packed piece of luggage. She lay quite still and tried to get it sorted out. Part of yesterday came gradually into shape. Every time she went over it in her mind the outline was more decided, the detail more apparent. From the moment when she stood in the dark, four steps up from a girl's murdered body, to the last conscious moment before she slipped into the darkness of sleep, it was all there. But back beyond that dark moment there was nothing. There was nothing at all. She didn't know who she was, or why she was here. There was cloud where there should have been memory. There was nothing but a dark cloud.

She pushed back the bedclothes, jumped out of bed, and went over to the window. The bright pale light of early morning was everywhere. She looked out onto a green lawn running down to great cedar trees. The air was fresh against her face, her neck, her uncovered arms. She looked down at herself and saw that she was wearing a pale pink nightgown. The sleeves and the neck were edged with lace. There was a blue ribbon run through a slotted insertion at the waist. A pale blue knitted jacket hung on the bottom rail of the bed, a pink ribbon to tie it. She put the blue jacket on. It felt warm and comfortable.

She got back into bed. These must be Lilian's clothes. Not Harriet's. Certainly not Harriet's. She began to wonder what Harriet's things would be like and pulled up from that to think with a breathless start, "What does it matter? What does anything matter except who I am and how did I get here?" A feeling of horror came over her — the old, old feeling of being lost in a strange world and not knowing where to put a foot. This that looked safe ground might crumble when you set foot upon it, the other that looked dry and stony could break suddenly and let the drowning waters through. For a moment she was beside herself with terror of the unknown. Then the swirling mists cleared and there came up in her strength and courage for the new day.

CHAPTER
SIX

She did not go to sleep again. She had no watch, but by the light she judged it to be something after six. She got her bag and counted the money in it. The inner compartment held ten one-pound notes. In the small outer purse there were a few pence, a sixpence, and a shilling, the remains of the loose spending money which she had broken into in the bus. She must have paid for her journey down here too. Yes — she could remember that. The other things in the bag were an ordinary pencil with a tin protector, bright green and not at all new, and a little calendar with a bunch of flowers on it in shades of pink and red, a pale yellow handkerchief without any mark on it.

The handkerchief sent her looking in the pockets of her coat and skirt. Thomasina had hung it in the wardrobe. It looked lonely there — made her seem to herself neglected, deserted — oh, she didn't know what. She shook the thought away and took down the coat and skirt. It was dark grey with a thread of blue in it, and the shirt was blue too. She went through the pockets of the coat and found nothing but a handkerchief — a blue handkerchief that matched the shirt. Her hat was on a shelf in the cupboard. Rather a nice hat, small and close — black and blue feathers. Just for a moment she came nearer to remembering when she had bought it and where, but it was gone again — no use thinking of it, no use trying to remember. Her shoes — black, neat, plain. Her stockings, nylon, fine mesh. She stopped with them in her hand. That was curious. Just for a moment she was buying stockings, and the girl was saying, "These are very nice," and she could hear herself say, "Oh, no, I want them finer than that." And then it was all gone again.

It shook her a little. She got back into bed, and presently Thomasina came in with a tray. She was in a silent mood. She put down the tray and was gone again without words. Anne got up and dressed.

It was when she was coming downstairs that Harriet came up behind her. She checked awkwardly, and then came on again with a curious slow reluctance. Anne said, "Good morning," and got rather a strange look in reply. She tried to describe it to herself afterwards and failed. It was half curious, half resentful. It seemed a long time before there was any answer, and when it came it was just a murmur that might have been anything. Harriet went past her at a run and was gone.

When she came down to the hall Anne was hesitating, not quite sure of the way. And then there was Lilian coming down behind her and full of talk.

"I hope you slept well. Sometimes one does after a journey, and sometimes one doesn't. My old nurse always said that what comes in your sleep the first night you're in a house sets the pattern, but of course that's all nonsense."

They crossed the hall and went into the dining room. There was porridge and a jug of milk, and tea in a fat old-fashioned teapot with a huge strawberry on the lid.

"I don't know what you have for breakfast. We just take porridge, but I believe the maids have eggs and bacon, so if you would like to ring, Thomasina will get you what you want. And then don't you think we should do something about finding your luggage? Where did you have it last?"

"I don't know —"

Lilian looked up from the careful ladling of porridge.

"There — that's yours. And the milk — we get very good milk here. And the sugar — do you take sugar?"

"No, thank you."

"Salt then — just by you. What were we talking about? Oh, yes, your luggage. Where did you have it last?"

"I don't — really know —"

Harriet came into the room, sat down opposite Anne, handled the letters, picked out two and opened one of them, becoming immediately absorbed in it.

Lilian prattled on.

"I always think it's a mistake to read letters at breakfast. My father never cared about our doing so. Of course he belonged to the generation that had the post brought in and put down in front of them, and no one expected to get their letters until he had gone through them. Now what was I saying when Harriet came in?

Oh, yes, it was about your things — your luggage. What did you say happened to them?"

"I don't know."

"Well, we must find out. When did you have them last?"

Anne felt a curious giddiness. She said, "I don't know —"

Lilian's tone sharpened.

"My dear, you must know when you last saw your own luggage!"

Harriet looked up from her letter and said, "Lucinda says everything is astonishingly dear."

This time Lilian took no notice of her. She repeated what she had said before.

"You must know when you saw your luggage last!"

"I — I'm afraid I don't."

"You got it off the boat?"

Nothing came to Anne's mind about getting her luggage off the boat. Nothing came to her about the boat, the voyage, her fellow travellers. She said humbly, "I don't seem to know anything at all."

Lilian looked at her in an odd way.

"How very singular. I don't think I should go about saying that to people. I don't know what you mean by it."

Anne said, "I don't know what I mean by it myself. I — I've lost my memory."

Harriet had lifted her head from her letter. A dark pale face with a startled look, her eyes oddly light.

"What do you mean?" she said.

Anne answered her.

30

"I don't remember anything before yesterday. I don't know why I have come here. I don't know who I am."

They were both looking at her now. There was something curious in the way of it. Lilian said slowly, "You don't know who you are?"

"No, I don't."

"Then how did you come by the bag and my letter?"

There was something in the tone, in the way that Lilian looked at her, that gave her pause. She opened her lips to reply and something struck them dumb again. Fear, doubt, caution — she didn't know which of these restrained her. Or was it something deeper? Something she didn't know about now — that she had known, and perhaps would know again? She didn't know it now. She put it away and said with an added firmness that surprised herself, "They were in my hand when I was walking down the street."

"And you don't know that you are Anne Fancourt?"

She shook her head and was silent for a moment. Then she said, "I'm Anne. I don't know about the Fancourt."

She could have said nothing more arresting. What Lilian knew, what Harriet knew, came to their minds. It was Harriet who said, "Don't you remember Jim?"

She shook her head. It was full of whirling thoughts. "No — no —"

It was Harriet who spoke again.

"Why, he's your husband!"

She felt herself in a strange place with an icy wind blowing. It went round, and round — round, and round. And then she was back in the room with Lilian and Harriet looking at her. She said, "I ought to have known that."

And Lilian said sharply, "Of course you ought! You had much better be quiet and try to remember!"

CHAPTER
SEVEN

Jim Fancourt looked out of the window and saw with his eyes the grey poplars and a flat monotony of fields, but he was not really aware of them. He was too busy with his thoughts, and they were too busy with the problem he had set them. He hoped Anne was all right. There wasn't any way of finding out short of running a risk, and there weren't going to be any more risks than he could help about this business. There had been too many already. He wondered how long they would have to wait for a divorce, and for the hundredth time wondered crossly how on earth he came to give way to Borrowdale. And then he was looking back, seeing Borrowdale's face with the desperate look on it and hearing his voice almost extinct, almost gone, "Get her — out of here — get her — away. For God's sake — do it — do it — do it."

Well, he had done it, and that was that. Borrowdale was dead, and Anne was alive and his wife — at least he supposed she was. He'd been a fool and he'd have to pay for it. Borrowdale was dead, and he'd made himself responsible for Anne. He could hardly remember her face. He could see the flat terror on it better than he could see the features. She hadn't made a fuss, but she had been terrified all right. And then Borrowdale had died, and the American plane had come down and he had got Anne on to it and it had got away. They would take her to London, and then she'd be all right.

Lilian and Harriet were not the most enlivening companions, but she'd be all right at Chantreys until he got there. He had given her a letter to post in town and told her where to go, and she ought to have been all right with Mrs Birdstock. She would have been all right in any case. What was he worrying about? He'd been a fool to concern himself with her at all. He pushed her into the back of his mind and began to think about Leamington. He would have to see him the minute he got to town, because he'd have to decide on the line they were going to take. It was immensely important. Anne came into that too. They could either scrap her altogether, leaving him to pick her up at Chantreys, or they could feature her — no, he didn't like that. He'd be hanged if he did. And it wouldn't fit in with the divorce. The whole thing made a properly straightforward story without her. Cut her out, keep her out — that was the way of it. Now as regards Leamington —

In about five minutes he was looking back at Anne and not remembering what she looked like. The picture came up in his mind. A little creature, brown eyes wild with fright, brown hair, a voice trembling with terror — and Borrowdale choking away his life. "Get her away — oh, my God — get her away —"

Nonsense! What was he at? He had got her away, hadn't he? If Borrowdale had had another day's life in him he might have known a little more about it. But it

34

wasn't so hard to make up a story of what he did know. She was Borrowdale's daughter — like enough to him for that to pass. And if, as he strongly suspected, her mother was Russian and there had never been a marriage, or not one that the Russians would admit — well, the rest followed easily enough. A Russian's daughter was a Russian, no matter whether she had an English father or not. That was their rule even where there had been a marriage, and it was ten to one there had been none in this case.

Looking back on it, he really didn't see why he had got himself into the mess. It had all been so hurried. Borrowdale gasping his life away after the rock had fallen, and the girl shaking with fright. A feeling of revulsion swept over him. What had it got to do with him after all? Marriage? Nonsense! It wouldn't hold water — not in England. He'd have to see a lawyer about it when he got home. The plane wouldn't have taken her if she hadn't sworn she was his wife.

He switched his mind to Leamington. What was he going to say to Leamington?

CHAPTER
EIGHT

Life went on for Anne. She had been for a week at Chantreys. Her memory had not come back. It began in the cellar of that house. It began with the murdered girl. For murdered she had been, of that she was quite sure. It was on the second day that the dreadful thought came to her. "Who murdered her? Was it I?" She didn't know the answer to that.

She went out and walked in the garden up and down the untidy autumn flower-beds, not seeing the Michaelmas daisies so nearly over, or the dahlias with their leaves crisped and blackened by the frost but the heads of them still shaggy and decorative, pink and yellow, crimson and white. She walked up and down, her hands clasped together as if they held something which if she let it go would be gone for ever, her thoughts trying to break through the curtain of fog which hung across the path. She tried it every way. She was Anne. She didn't know her surname. She didn't know what she had been doing, or why she was in town, or who the dead girl was. She didn't know what she had been doing all her life until now. She didn't know who she was. It always came round to that.

She tried again. She was Anne. That was the only thing she felt sure about. She wasn't sure about being Anne Fancourt. But she was Anne, she did know that. She didn't know who the dead girl was. She didn't know whom the bag belonged to — was it hers, or was it the dead girl's? She didn't *know* whose it was. If it was hers, she was Anne Fancourt — she was Mrs James Fancourt. Could you be married and have no recollection, not the slightest, faintest gleam? You wouldn't think so. You wouldn't think it would be possible to forget being married. Coldly and deliberately her own mind answered her. It had happened again, and again, and again. She didn't know how she knew that, but she did know it. A shock — she must have had a shock. That was what made you lose your memory — a shock, or a blow on the head. She didn't think she had had a blow. But a shock — anyone can have a shock. You read about people in the papers who had some kind of shock and who forgot who they were.

She stood quite still, and the clasp of her hands tightened. Had she left father and mother, a family, brothers, sisters, to become — she didn't know what or who? No, she mustn't think that way. Could you forget a family as easily as that? She didn't think so — she wouldn't think so. Deep down in her, almost unknown, was something very strong. If she had had father, mother, brothers, sisters, she wouldn't have forgotten them. She couldn't have had them. It was like brushing against something incalculable, uncertain. Gone in a moment of time, but even as it went, it left her strengthened, though she didn't know why.

She began to walk again, and the thoughts went on and on. They beat against the fog and came back to her. Who was she? She was Anne. Anne who? She didn't know. The more she thought of it, the less she knew. She stopped thinking then.

But if you stop thinking, you are really dead. She turned round. She wasn't dead, she was alive. She had got to think this thing out. She started again. She was Anne — that was the one thing to be sure of. According to the evidence of the handbag she was Anne Fancourt, and she was married to Jim Fancourt. She hadn't the slightest recollection of being married. But she had no recollection of the past at all. Her life began, her conscious life began, when she stood on the cellar steps and looked down on a girl's dead body. She had not then any idea who the girl might be. She only knew that she must get away from her. And then the second thought that had come — "You can't go away like that. Oh, no, you can't!" and she had taken the torch out of the bag and gone down and looked. There was the wound in the head. At the memory of it she turned cold and sick. No one with a wound like that could be alive — but she had stooped to the ungloved hand — and the hand was cold. She could not control the violent shudder that shook her as she remembered the cold and clammy feeling of that dead hand.

She remembered everything from there — how she had put out the light and listened, and how there had been no sound, and how she had come up the steps into the dark entrance hall, and so out into the street, and along it until she had come to the bus. Miss Silver

38

wasn't on the bus when she got on to it. She could see the bus quite clearly. It had stopped and she had got on to it, and then it had gone on again. She had shut her eyes, and when she opened them Miss Silver was there, sitting opposite to her in a neat shabby black coat and a much newer hat with a half-wreath of red roses on one side and an odd trimming of black chiffon rosettes on the other. The rosettes and the flowers grew smaller as they drew together in front of the hat.

She pulled herself up sharply. What was the good of thinking about Miss Silver's hat? She was never likely to see it or her again. If she was to think, let her for goodness' sake think about something or someone useful.

She must think about Jim Fancourt. She must think about the man who might be her husband. If she was Anne Fancourt, that was what he was. It lay between her and the dead girl at the foot of the stairs. The bag with the letter to Anne Fancourt in it had been on a level with her, and she had been some steps up. She had had to open the bag to get out the torch by which she had seen the dead girl. How did she know there was a torch there if it wasn't her bag? The letter from Lilian was in her bag. If the bag was hers, she was Anne Fancourt, Jim Fancourt's wife, and a niece of Lilian and Harriet. If it wasn't hers, but the dead girl's, then it was that dead girl who was Anne Fancourt.

Up and down, to and fro, endlessly, timelessly. The light changed, deepened, turned to grey. A little shudder went over her. It was no good going on thinking.

She turned and went back to the house.

CHAPTER
NINE

It was two days later that she spoke to Lilian.

"You said you had a letter about me from Jim. Might I see it?"

Lilian stared at her, a little offended as it seemed.

"Well, I don't know. Yes, I suppose so — if you really want to. I think I kept it."

Something like a half-struck match went off in the darkness of Anne's mind. There wasn't time for her to see anything by the light of it, but there was something there to be seen, she was sure about that. It was gone in a flash, but it had been there. She said, "It might help me to remember, if you don't mind."

Lilian had gone over to her writing-table. She opened a drawer and began to fuss over the papers that were in it.

"Miss Porson . . . dear, dear, I must remember to write. And Mary Jacks . . . One really ought not to put letters away, one forgets them so dreadfully. Now where did I . . . Oh, here's the recipe for that very good apple-chutney we had at Miss Maule's. I am pleased about that. I'll leave it out and give it to Mattie. She's so much better at remembering things than I am. Now what was it I was looking for . . . Oh, yes, Jim's letter about your coming. Now you wouldn't think I would have thrown that away, would you? I wonder if it wasn't in this drawer at all. What do you think? Shall I finish this drawer and then go on to the one underneath it, where it is really much more likely to be, and I can't think why I didn't look there first. What do you think?"

Anne said, "I don't know. I think I should finish one drawer at a time."

Lilian sat back and looked at her.

"Ah, that is the way the ordinary person looks for anything, but if you are guided by intuition it is all so much simpler, and intuition tells me — now what does it tell me?"

Anne said, "I don't know. I wish I did."

Miss Lilian bundled all the papers from her lap back into the drawer.

"My intuition tells me that this next drawer may be the one." She began to take out the papers and put them in piles. "Three catalogues of garden seeds. Now how did these get in here? I can't think. And really, you know, we never have got garden seeds from anyone but Hodgson. I think I must tear these up. Or perhaps not . . . Oh, there's Ramsbottom's bill! My dear, you are doing me quite a good turn! I've been looking for that, and it's really got no business in this drawer. I can't think how I came to put it there. Let me see — what were we looking for? Jim's last letter — yes, yes, I must keep hold of that and not let myself be distracted. Jim's letter — oh, yes, here it is! You wanted to see it, didn't you?" She held out a sheet of paper and then drew it back again. "I don't know whether I ought to show it to you. You can't be too careful. My friend Mrs Kesteven knew someone who showed a letter to her daughter-in-law, and it wasn't from her husband at all. No, I think I've got that wrong, but it doesn't matter, because the principle remains the same — never show letters. Not that there is anything in this one, so perhaps you had better read it." She held the letter out again and Anne took it from her.

It felt strange in her hand. It shouldn't do that. Everything about it was strange. Utterly strange. The handwriting nice. Clear. Firm. But she had never seen it before. As she looked down at it she felt quite sure about that. But that might be true, and yet the man who had written it might be her husband, because hidden behind a wall of mist in her mind was all the story of her marriage.

For a moment everything seemed to press on her. She felt giddy, and looked round for a chair. When she had found one she sank on to it, passed her hand across her eyes, pressing on them hard. After a moment they cleared. She was aware of Lilian looking at her. She couldn't tell with what expression, but it came to her afterwards that it was curiosity, suspicion, she didn't know what. She made her eyes focus on the paper and read:

Dear Lilian

I think I shall be home almost as soon as this gets to you, which it will do by means of my wife. I have married rather suddenly, and have taken the opportunity of shipping her off by an American plane which came down here. Better not talk about this, as it's a bit of a job. They came down for temporary repairs, and were good enough to take Anne along. I calculate I should be home by the end of the month. Everything when we meet.

Yours,

J.F.

She read it twice. It meant nothing to her at all. When she looked up and saw that Lilian was watching her — she had been watching her all the time she had been reading the letter — she had a moment of acute fear. It came, caught her, and obliterated thought, sense, everything. It was like being pounced upon by some strange animal in a nightmare. She didn't know what she was afraid of, or why she was afraid.

Lilian's rather high voice came to her as if from a distance. She could only just hear it.

"Good gracious, Anne, what is the matter?"

She heard her own voice say with the same effect of distance, "I don't know."

"Anne — are you all right?"

The nightmare feeling left her. She was able to say, "Yes — thank you —"

She could see Lilian's face now — curious. She said, "I don't know why — as if —" Her voice tailed away.

"Well, as you are all right now — you're sure you are all right? You're very pale."

"Yes, I'm quite all right. It was just —"

Lilian looked at her. There was something curious in her expression.

"You haven't really forgotten Jim, have you?"

"I don't know how long I knew him." There was uncertainty in her voice.

Lilian gave her little high laugh.

"You will have quite a tidying up to do when he comes — won't you?"

CHAPTER
TEN

It was two days later that Jim Fancourt came. Anne was in the garden. She heard the sound of a car. It went past her on the other side of the hedge. She felt nothing. Oh, no — nothing at all. That seemed very curious to think about afterwards, but at the time it seemed quite natural. She didn't even think about it, but went on tidying up the border. There was a gardener, but he was an old man, and in his time the garden had had three men to do the work. Wherever she had been for all the unknown years, she had known all about clearing up a border. She didn't have to think about that. Her hands remembered, if she had forgotten. When she heard steps behind her on the garden path she took them for the old gardener's and said, "These chrysanthemums have done well — haven't they? They must like the soil here."

The voice that was not the gardener's said from behind her, "Oh, they do."

She looked over her shoulder and saw Jim Fancourt. There was a moment in which she didn't know who he was, and another moment when she knew. In between those two moments there was a feeling as if she was drowning. She had nearly drowned when she was ten years old. It came back to her vividly. They were in a boat, and the boat was upset. She was in water — deep, deep water. And then through the fear and the drowning there had come a voice — hands — and she was saying . . .

She got up slowly and faced him. He was tall — that was the first impression. And then she saw that he was frowning.

He said short and sharp, "Who are you?" and she gave him the only answer she could.

"I don't know — if you don't."

The frown deepened.

"And what do you mean by that?"

She made a helpless gesture.

"I don't know — anything."

"What do you mean?"

"Just what I said."

There was a moment's pause before he said, "You're not going to faint, are you?"

She shook her head.

"I don't think so. I — I'd like to sit down."

He gave a half laugh.

"There's the potting-shed — can you get as far as that?"

She nodded, and moved. The next thing she knew was an arm about her, a feeling of support, not unwelcome. She shut her eyes, was conscious of being guided, and of returning consciousness. The voice said, "Here we are. Untidy old man, Clarke. Can you stand for a minute whilst I get all these sacks to one end of the seat? Now — sit down! Feel better?"

She opened her eyes and said, "Yes — thank you —"

Those opened eyes of hers were like two open windows. The thought went through his mind — two windows open, and someone there not knowing that she was being looked at. He turned round quickly, walked to the door of the potting-shed, checked himself, and walked back again. He said, "Do you know who I am?"

"I think so —".

"Well?"

"You are Jim Fancourt, aren't you?"

"I am."

Something came over her, she didn't know what it was. She got to her feet and stood there, leaning forward a little, her hands holding each other tightly, her eyes fixed on his face. They stood there looking at one another. He had no consciousness of ever having seen her before. They were strangers. She did not know him, nor did he know her. But underneath all that there was a deep, strong pull. He didn't know what it was, but it was there. He said in a rough voice, "Who are you?"

Her eyes were wide. They seemed to search his face. She said in a toneless whisper, "I'm Anne —"

"Anne who? Anne what?"

"I — don't — know —"

She thought he was going to leave her, for he turned and went out of the shed.

She sat down on the bench again and closed her eyes. Time ceased. And then her hand was taken and he was there quite close to her, sitting on the bench, his warm hand holding hers. His voice, strong and firm, seemed to come from a long way off. It wasn't kind or unkind, it was just a voice. It wasn't angry. Perhaps it was too far off to be angry. She didn't know. The voice said, "You're Anne?"

"I'm Anne." It was the one thing she was sure about.

"You're not the Anne I was looking for."

There was a lonely wind blowing. It cut her off from everyone else in the world. She didn't belong to anyone.

"I'm not?"

"Didn't you know that?"

She was looking at him again. She said, "No, I didn't know."

"What do you mean by that?"

"I don't — know —"

The hand that was holding hers increased its warm, strong pressure. He said, "Look here, what is all this? You came here. You had Anne's bag. What does it all mean? You've got to tell me!"

"Yes —"

If she told him, would he believe her? There was so little to tell — so very, very little. Would anyone believe she was telling all she knew? She went on looking at him, but she didn't really see him. Not as he saw her.

She said, "It's all dark — up to a point. I'll tell you what I can. I don't see why you should believe me, but I'll tell you —" She paused for so long that it was as if a tap had been turned on and no water flowed from it. And then, just as he was going to say something, she began to speak. "It was quite dark. Quite, quite dark. I thought I was going to faint. I was standing on some steps. I sat down. I put my head on my knees. The faintness went away. I was on steps. I knew that. I knew I had come down the steps and dropped my bag. I knew that someone was lying dead at the bottom of the steps. I don't know how I knew it, but I did."

She stopped, and there was a silence. When he said, "Go on," she began again.

"The bag was on the steps beside me — I thought it was mine." The hand that was clasped in his twitched, and she said more earnestly and naturally than she had spoken yet, "I did think that. I thought it was my bag, and that I had dropped it there on the steps."

He said, "Yes —" His voice gave her some reassurance, she didn't know how or why. When he said, "Go on," it was suddenly easier. She began to tell him about taking the torch out of the bag and switching it on.

"It was there — in the bag. I switched it on and saw her. She was lying on the floor at the bottom of the steps. I knew that she was dead."

He said quick and sharp, "How did you know that? Did you kill her?"

She said in a surprised voice, "Oh, no, I didn't — I'm quite sure I didn't! Why should I?"

"I don't know."

She said with the simplicity of one who explains to a small child, "I couldn't have done it. There wasn't anything to do it with."

"How do you know that?"

"I could see. There wasn't anything there to shoot her with. There wasn't anything at all — there really wasn't."

He found himself believing her. It wasn't the words, it was something else — something in her look, in her voice.

"Go on."

"I went down. I felt her wrist. It was quite cold. There was some broken glass — it was from the other torch —"

"What other torch?"

"I think it was mine."

She was aware of his eyes on her, steady and level — not accusing, not believing — just waiting. She went on.

"I can't remember, but I think — I think I must have come down the steps before. I think it was my torch that I had when I saw her."

"But you can't remember?"

"No, I can't — remember —"

"Go on."

"I went down. The other torch was there — broken — on the ground. I had the feeling it was mine. I don't know if it was really."

"Well?"

She said with the most touching simplicity, "I felt her hand. It was quite cold."

"How do you know she was dead? Anyone who is in a faint may be cold."

She pulled her hand away from him, and put both hands over her eyes.

"Why do you make me say it? She had been shot from behind. Her head — oh —"

"You're sure she was dead?"

She dropped her hands from her eyes and said, "Oh, yes, I'm sure — quite sure. Nobody could be alive with a wound like that."

There was a pause. He believed her. He didn't know why, but he did believe her. He got up, walked to the door of the shed, and stood there. When he turned his manner had changed. He said, "How much have you told them here?"

"Nothing."

She felt as if he was looking through and through her.

"Why?"

"I kept thinking — perhaps I should — remember —"

"Well, go on. What did you do?"

"I came up the steps."

"With the light in your hand?"

"No — I put it out."

"Why?"

"I was afraid."

"Of what?"

"That someone had killed her."

"Who else was in the house?"

"I don't know."

She was looking at him all the time.

"What did you do?"

"The hall was dark — the front door wasn't quite shut — I came out into the street —"

"What street?"

She shook her head.

"I don't know. It was quiet — dark. It went into a street with buses. I got into a bus. It brought me to the station."

"What made you come here?"

"There was a Miss Silver — she was in the bus —"

"Miss Silver?"

Something in his tone surprised her. She said, "Do you know her?"

"What is she like?"

She turned her thoughts back.

"She's small — not young — old-fashioned looking — like the governess out of an old-fashioned story book. She was very kind and — and — practical. She had on a black coat and a kind of a fur tippet, and a hat with red roses on one side and little sort of whisks of black net on the other. I think she saw that I didn't know what to do. She took me into the station to have tea, and I told her all about it." She stopped there with an air of finality. She had told him what she knew. Now it was for him to do something about it.

He sat in frowning silence. If this was true? He believed that it was true. He couldn't say why, but he did believe it. His thoughts strayed off to Miss Silver. He had met her. She was a friend of Frank Abbott's. He could check up with her. He didn't really need to. He could feel the girl straining to tell the truth as she saw it. It was a very queer business — very queer indeed.

CHAPTER
ELEVEN

They came back towards the house. There was no more said. She had a curious feeling of relief. She hadn't to think any more, or plan, or be troubled. It was his business, and he was fully able for it.

When they were still some way from the house he stopped her, his right hand on her arm.

"Wait a minute — we've got to say the same thing."

Those clear eyes of hers looked up at him. When he saw that she wasn't going to speak, he said, "We've got to say the same thing. I had to send you here — that is, I had to send Anne —"

"If I'm not Anne, you didn't send me." The words came out a mere statement of fact. Behind the calmness of her tone there was a dreadful void feeling. If she wasn't Anne, who was she? The answer to that came fast and breathless, "I am Anne." There must be thousands and thousands of Annes in the world. She was one of them, if she wasn't Anne Fancourt.

He said, "Look here —" He stopped, and then began all over again. "You haven't said anything about this to Lilian and Harriet?"

She went on looking at him with those clear eyes. She said, "No," and then, after a pause, "I didn't know

— I didn't remember. I thought perhaps I might remember —" Her voice faded out.

He said, "Then I think it would be best just to go on in the same way. I shan't be staying, so it won't be difficult for you. I must try and find out what has happened to her."

She said, still looking at him, "She was dead — she was really dead."

"Don't you see I must prove that? If she was dead, who killed her and why, poor girl?"

She said, "Will you tell me about her? Who was she?"

He frowned suddenly.

"She was Anne Borrowdale. She was with her father in —" He paused and said, "I'd better not say where. We had no business to be there really. No, I don't know that I can tell you any more — I think better not. Her father was killed accidentally, and right on that an American plane came down — and you'd better not say anything about that either, because they'd got no business there. Bad weather, and they were a hundred miles off their course. They came down, put her right, and got off again. They took Anne with them, as my wife. There — that's the story. And you keep mum about it until I tell you! Do you see?"

"Yes."

The curious thing was that her one word carried such conviction. He went on.

"I've got to try and trace her."

"What will you do?"

He was wondering about that, but as soon as she spoke he knew.

54

"I shall see Miss Silver."

She made a little doubtful movement of her head.

"I don't know that that will help. What can she do?"

"She can tell me where she got on the bus."

"Yes — she can do that. But would that help?"

"I don't know. It might."

They walked along in silence. It wasn't the strained, awkward silence that it might have been. Each thought of that. It was more like the companionable silence of two people who do not speak because there is no need to speak, because they have confidence in one another. Neither of them knew that the other had this feeling. Each had it so strongly that it sufficed without words.

They came down out of the garden and across a spread of lawn to where he had left his car before he spoke again. Then he said, "Will you tell them I couldn't wait? They'll think it odd, but no odder than most of the things I've done in the last ten years."

She said, "I'll tell them," and stood to see him get in and drive away.

When he was almost out of sight, Lilian came out of the house.

"He's not gone? Oh, he can't be gone! You haven't let him go!"

Anne came back from a long way off to say gravely and simply, "He had to go."

"But why? I don't understand at all — why has he gone?"

Anne said, "I don't know. He didn't tell me."

She got a sharp look for that.

"Have you quarrelled?"

"Oh, no!"

There was genuine surprise in her voice. There hadn't been time for them to quarrel. She had the feeling as she spoke that, with all the time in the world, there would be no time for them to quarrel in.

Lilian had come close up to her.

"I don't understand you at all, Anne. Your husband comes down here. We are expecting him, naturally. I tell him you are in the garden, and he says he will go out and find you. And now you tell me he has gone! I don't understand it at all!"

Anne roused herself. It was all rather like a dream. But she mustn't let Lilian be angry if she could help it — she wasn't sure that she could help it. She said, "He asked me things. When I told him, he said he had better see about them at once. He said to tell you."

"Things!" said Lilian angrily. "I can't imagine what you mean! I can't imagine what he means! It all sounds nonsense to me — perfect nonsense!"

CHAPTER
TWELVE

Miss Silver had not forgotten her encounter with the girl who might or might not be Mrs James Fancourt. It had occurred to her more than once that she would like to know what had happened, and whether her memory had come back. But she had restrained herself. She had been partly helped in this restraint by the fact that not only was she very busy with the tail end of the Lena Morrison business, but she had also been concerned about, and her thoughts a good deal taken up by, the accident to her niece Ethel Burkett's youngest child, Josephine, who had slipped on the kerb just opposite their house and contracted so badly bruised an ankle that for three days there had been doubts as to whether it had not been broken. This was now happily a thing of the past. The Morrison affair was practically done with, and there was nothing to prevent Miss Silver from giving her full attention to a new appeal for her help.

She had just finished a letter in which she had poured out her thankfulness over the happy outcome of Josephine's accident, when the telephone bell rang at her elbow. She picked it up, said "Miss Silver speaking," and heard a voice in reply.

"Miss Silver, can you see me now? It's rather important."

"Who is it?"

"I'm sorry — I ought to have begun with that. I'm Jim Fancourt. We met last year. I know Frank Abbott."

"Of course — I remember you very well. Are you in town?"

"Yes. I wondered if I could come and see you now."

"Yes, do."

As she hung up she remembered Anne Fancourt and wondered.

When twenty minutes later the bell rang, she had reviewed her interview with Anne, and whilst she abstained from linking her with Jim Fancourt who was Frank Abbott's friend, she was nevertheless prepared for any eventuality.

Jim Fancourt was ushered in upon a peaceful scene. The peacock-blue curtains were drawn across the windows. There was a pleasant little fire upon the hearth. Miss Silver had risen to greet him from a comfortable fireside chair. She wore a dark blue dress, and without her hat displayed a quantity of brown hair lightly tinged with grey and arranged after a fashion which reminded him vaguely of the family album which his grandfather had had lying on the big round table in the drawing-room.

Miss Silver shook hands with him, pointed him to another fireside chair, and sat down. She was knitting what appeared to be a shawl in a pale shade of pink.

He sat down, leaned forward, and said directly, "Miss Silver, do you mind if I ask you some questions?

I know from Frank Abbott that you are absolutely to be relied upon."

Miss Silver looked up at him. She said, "Yes, Mr Fancourt."

He said at once, "I've been out in the Middle East. Part of the time I was where I wasn't supposed to be. There was another man there called Borrowdale. I went there to meet him. He had his daughter with him. Borrowdale met with an accident — no proof as to whether it really was an accident or not — a loose stone on a hillside —" He broke off and shrugged Borrowdale away. "Well, there you have it. He lived for twenty-four hours, and the one thing he wanted was to get his daughter away. She was there with him, and I think from what he said that her mother was Russian and he wasn't too sure that the marriage would hold water when it came to a passport. He asked me to get her away, and I said I would do what I could. Well, he died. Then an American plane came down. I said the girl was my wife, and asked them to take her along and keep quiet about it. Well, they did. Meanwhile I'd finished my job, and I got over the border and took a plane home. I'd given the girl a letter to my relations at Haleycott. I have just come from there now. I expect you know why I wanted to see you."

Miss Silver had been knitting as he spoke. Now, without stopping, she said, "Yes, Mr Fancourt?" in the tone which invites a continuance.

He made a quick gesture with his hands.

"Well, I've come here to ask you for every detail of your meeting with Anne."

Miss Silver took her time. She knitted a whole row before she answered him. Then she said, "You are asking me about my meeting with Anne Fancourt?"

He shook his head.

"She's not Anne Fancourt — I know that. Since you've talked to her, you must know that she doesn't say that she is Anne Fancourt, she only says she is Anne. I'd like to know what else she said."

Miss Silver was again silent for a moment. When she did speak it was with gravity and deliberation. She stopped knitting and rested her hands upon the half-completed pink shawl.

"I caught my bus at 6.45. She was there already. I could not help noticing her. She had a shocked look.

"When we reached Victoria I waited a little. I was concerned for her. She appeared to me to have sustained a shock. I wished to be sure that she knew where she was and what she was going to do. Almost at once I was sure that she did not know, and I ventured to speak to her. It at once became obvious that she did not know either where she was or where she was going. I took her to the refreshment-room and ordered tea. It was obvious that she had been gently reared. She was at the same time faint with hunger and carefully observant of the delicacies of her social behaviour. I formed the opinion that it was some time since she had tasted food, and I put her exhausted condition down to this fact."

"Why should she have been without food?"

"I cannot tell you. She had with her a bag, black lined with grey and with a centre partition. There was a

60

small purse high up on the right-hand side. It contained a little change, but in the inner compartment there was ten pounds in notes."

Jim Fancourt nodded.

"I gave her ten pounds in English money," he said. "She hadn't any bag when I saw her."

"Then she had bought one. It was quite new. There was a handkerchief in it, and a mirror. The handkerchief was also new. It had not been washed, and there was no name on it. She took out a letter. She read it and gave it to me to read. It was from Miss Fancourt, and it said that it was very difficult to know how to write, but that they had had your letter and would do what you asked and take her in. It went on to say that it was all very worrying, that your letter was very short and did not really tell them anything except that you had married her, and that she would be arriving. And it finished up by saying that it all seemed very strange but of course they would do what they could, and that they did not at all understand why you had not come over with her. When she gave me the letter she said, 'I don't know what it means.' When I said, 'How did this reach you?' she said she did not know. I told her that she ought to go to the address at the head of the letter. I said she was expected, and that if she did not come, there would be anxiety. I added that she might wake up in the morning and find that everything was clear again. I have known of such cases. Am I to understand that her memory has not cleared up?"

He said, "No, it hasn't. She can't remember who she is. She's not the girl to whom Lilian wrote that letter.

61

She's not Anne Fancourt at all. I've never seen her until this afternoon, but the letter in her bag was Anne's — I mean the girl I was looking for."

"Your wife?"

"I don't know if she was my wife or not. Borrowdale — her father — he made us promise — he was dying —" He ran a hand through his hair. "It all sounds positively lunatic now."

Miss Silver had picked up her knitting again. She said, "Things that sound very strange in one set of circumstances may appear perfectly reasonable in another."

He gave a short laugh.

"You've said it! Well, an American plane came down — they'd got a hundred miles off their route. I told the pilot my wife had had a shock and I wanted to get her out of there. He was a light-hearted fellow, and they took her along. I had a bit of luck and got across — well, I won't say where. When I got down to Haleycott, there was Anne, and she wasn't the right Anne. I'd never seen her before in my life, and she'd lost her memory." He leaned forward and said, "How much did she tell you?"

"What I have just told you."

He leaned back again.

"She told me more than that. She said the first thing she remembered was being on some steps. She said it was all dark up to a point — quite, quite dark — and that she thought she was going to faint, so she sat down. She was on steps, and she was faint. She said she knew she was on the steps and that she had dropped

62

her bag. It was on the steps beside her — she thought it was hers. She must have taken up the bag and opened it, because presently she had a torch. She switched it on and saw a girl lying on the floor at the bottom of the steps. I asked her, 'How did you know she was dead? Did you kill her?' She said in a surprised sort of way, 'Oh, no, I didn't — I'm quite sure I didn't! Why should I?' And then she said, as if it explained everything, 'I couldn't have done it — there wasn't anything to do it with.'" He broke off, looked at Miss Silver, and said, "It was very convincing. I found I was believing her. It wasn't what she said, it was something about her."

Miss Silver looked at him and smiled. She said, "I know."

He went on to tell her the rest of it.

"She said the other girl had been shot from behind. She had been shot in the head. She was quite sure she was dead. And she was quite sure she hadn't shot her. She said, 'I couldn't have done it — there wasn't anything there to do it with.' She said she went down the steps, and the other girl was there, and she was dead." He stopped and ran his hands through his hair. "I'm telling it very badly. I don't know — I can't see how it hangs together. She said she went down the steps with the torch she took out of the bag, and there was this girl in the cellar, and she was quite dead. I don't know whether it was Anne or not. It seems as if it must have been, but the only thing that makes it seem like that is the letter — Lilian's letter to Anne. That's really the only clue."

"And you haven't seen it."

"No, I've only got your account of it." He gave a short impatient laugh. "It's the sort of letter Lilian would write!"

CHAPTER
THIRTEEN

Jim Fancourt leaned forward suddenly.

"We'll have to try and find the house."

Miss Silver looked at him.

"I can't see any other way," he said.

"How do you propose to find it?"

He began to speak, not as if he was talking to her, but rather as if he was thinking aloud.

"If it's an empty house it won't be so difficult. To be used for a murder like that, the house would either be empty or the people would be away — or else they'd be the tenants, I don't think that's so very likely. No, I should think it lay between the first two — either a dead empty house, or one where the people are away. Yes, that'll be it." He changed his tone and spoke directly to Miss Silver. "I've been down to the people Anne stayed with — or rather she didn't stay with them. I didn't like to send her straight to my aunts in case of their not being able to have her. They might have been away, or something like that. So I gave her the address of an old parlourmaid who lets rooms. She was to go there, forward my letter to Lilian, and wait for an answer. Well, she did that — at least she did part of it. She didn't stay there. She must have posted my

65

letter to Lilian, and she called for the answer. At least someone called for it on the morning of the day that you saw Anne in the bus. That Anne reached Haleycott the same evening. The real Anne was murdered between the time she fetched the letter and the time that the other Anne stumbled on her in the cellar of that house."

Miss Silver said, "Dear me!" Then she said, "Do you think that it was the real Anne who fetched the letter?"

"I don't know. It might have been — it might not. Mrs Birdstock is short-sighted, and it was a dark morning. She says the lady rang the bell and said she was Mrs Fancourt. Was there a letter for her, please? She was expecting one. Mrs Birdstock says she did have a good look at her then, but she was standing with her back to the light and she couldn't make much of it. She says she was young and quite pretty, and it never entered her head that there was anything wrong, so she gave her the letter. She says the young lady opened it and read it then and there, and when Mrs Birdstock asked her if there was anything she could do for her she just said no, thank you, she would be going straight down to Haleycott, and that was all. She went away with the letter which was found in Anne's bag. And whether she was really Anne or not, no one knows. If she was, why didn't she go straight to Mrs Birdstock and stay there until she heard from Lilian, which was what she had been told to do? She hadn't done that, you know. You have to allow three days to get an answer to a letter from London. If she wrote to Haleycott one day, Lilian would get it the next day, and if she wrote at once in reply — well, you see how it goes."

Miss Silver said, "Yes."

"Then there's another thing. The letter Lilian wrote was found in her bag. The girl who called on Mrs Birdstock hadn't a bag at all. When she had read the letter she put it in the pocket of her coat. She hadn't got a bag. Mrs Birdstock noticed that most particularly. She may not have been Anne at all. But if she wasn't, who was she? Someone who was sent to get that letter? I don't know, you don't know, nobody knows. There's no sense in it."

Miss Silver put the pink shawl into a knitting-bag which she had placed on the lower shelf of the table beside her. All her movements were without fuss or hurry. When she had disposed of the bag she said, "I will put on my hat and coat. We will see whether we can identify the house."

She came back into the room a few minutes later in the black coat and the fur tippet which Anne had described. She wore black thread gloves and a neat pair of black Oxford shoes, but instead of the hat with the red roses she was wearing a very similar shape with a bow of black ribbon on one side and a bunch of small mixed flowers upon the other.

As they went on their way she was thinking intently of her interview with Anne. When she had entered the bus Anne was already sitting on the opposite side of it with a lost look which had immediately attracted her attention. She had no idea how long she had been sitting there. There was no means of knowing.

They rode for one more street, and then Miss Silver got out. When Jim Fancourt had followed her, they were standing at the corner. She turned to him and said, "It *may* be this street. We have no means of knowing."

"She might have crossed over. The road we want may be on the other side."

Miss Silver shook her head.

"I do not think it likely. She was not in a state to do anything except what was obvious. I think she would have reached the main road and got onto the first bus that came along. She was in a dazed condition and faint with hunger."

He said, "Why?" his voice angry.

"I do not know. It was certainly hours since she had eaten."

They began to walk down the street. They walked all down one side and up the other. There was no house to let or with the appearance of being unoccupied. It was the next turning which held out the first hope. Half-way down it there stood an unmistakably empty house. There was a board up which said "Briggs & Co." and the address on the board was round the corner on the main road.

Miss Silver strolled on the opposite side whilst Jim Fancourt went for the key. He came back accompanied by a golden-haired young man with a ready tongue.

"The late Miss Kentish's house," he explained. "The family have left the furniture here for the time being. It is a most comfortable residence and has been well looked after. Very particular Miss Kentish was. How many bedrooms did you want, madam? Five or six? You would, I think, find the accommodation just what you require. Of course a house does not show at its best when it has been shut up for six months — you will quite appreciate that, I am sure." He put a key in the door, turned it, and the cold, still air of the house came to meet them.

Jim Fancourt had cause to think of Miss Silver with gratitude. She was so perfectly at her ease. She produced a pencil and paper and took notes. She brimmed over with the right questions and took down the answers so readily supplied by the golden-haired young man.

They went all over the house and found nothing at all until they came back to the empty echoing hall. There Miss Silver lingered.

"The kitchen —" she said. "The friend who told me about the house mentioned it particularly. I hope it is on the ground floor. I do not like basement kitchens at all, and I am afraid —"

The young man broke in brightly.

"Ah, madam, your views are exactly the same as those of the late Miss Kentish. She had a horror of a basement, and built out at the back."

He led the way. The kitchen was neat and spotless. Having viewed it and the scullery, they came back again to the hall. It was dark there. Jim Fancourt moved restlessly. The young man continued to speak of the convenience, the comfort, the good furnishing of the house. "I am sure you would find it just what you want," he was saying, when Jim broke in.

"I should like to see the cellar."

"Oh, of course — of course," said the young man. "But I'm afraid there is no lighting. Miss Kentish did not use it, so omitted to install the electric light."

He went past them and opened a door. It was not easily seen. There was a screen which had to be pushed away. A table stood close in to it. The young man from the office found himself tired, but he continued with his role of persevering politeness.

"There is nothing here," he said, "but it would of course make a capital place for the storage of heavy luggage."

Jim said, "I should like to go down. I have a torch. There is no need for you to bother." He produced from his pocket a small but powerful torch and turned it on.

Miss Silver stepped after him into the open door. The voice of the young man followed them as they descended the steps.

"There is really nothing down there — nothing at all."

They took no notice of him. Miss Silver came down slowly. She had made no picture of what she expected to see. What she did see in the concentrated torch-light was a clean, bare floor at the foot of the steps. It was quite clean, quite bare.

It was too clean, too bare.

The house was clean. The bright young man had laid stress on that. A woman came once a week to open the windows and to dust. Miss Silver thought she must be a prodigy unique amongst charwomen if she descended into the cellar and extended her ministrations to its floor.

70

The cellar was entirely empty except for two or three boards which leaned against the wall on the far side. Jim Fancourt stood in the middle of the bare floor space and shone his light upon it. There was a dead silence. Then he pushed the torch into Miss Silver's hand and went to move the clutter of old boards against the wall. There was nothing behind them — no gap in the wall, no door. But on Miss Silver's exclamation he turned round to her and saw that she was pointing. A small bright bead lay on the floor where the dust behind the boards had not been cleared. There was thick dust, and that small bright bead no larger than a pea. He stooped to pick it up and stood there, the bead in his hand and the light of the torch upon it.

Miss Silver spoke in a low voice.

"Why is it not dusty like the floor?"

Jim Fancourt frowned. The small bead lay on his palm. There was no dust on it. He moved his hand, and the bead on the palm moved. He did not speak, but he stooped down and touched the floor outside the space where the boards had been piled. There was no dust outside, no dust at all. Under the shelter of the boards which he had just moved there was a soft thick layer which spoke of years of neglect. But the bead itself was clean. The months or years during which the dust had gathered had not troubled its brightness. If it had lain there for those months or years, the dust would have silted into it and over it and through it. It had lain there no more than a few days. It was a witness. His mind went back to Anne as he had seen her just before she

71

stepped into the plane and left him. She had about her neck a chain of little beads like this one. He put the bead away in his pocket.

As they came up the cellar steps Miss Silver did all the talking. She thanked the young man and said they would have to ask the lady for whom they were acting.

"Oh, no, it is not for ourselves. We shall have to let my sister know, but I am afraid the house may be a little too large for her, and she did not really wish to take a furnished house."

"The furniture could be removed," said the young man with bright hopefulness.

"Ah, well. I will let you know if she thinks that this will suit her, but I am very much afraid —"

When the young man had taken his departure they walked on to the far end of the road in silence. As they turned to come back Miss Silver spoke.

"You recognise the bead?"

"Yes."

"It was Anne's?"

"Yes."

He walked beside her in silence until they came to the house again. Then he said, "The bead was from a necklace she wore. She wore it always. This means that the other Anne's story is true — not just a dream or anything like that. She did see a girl's dead body in that cellar. It doesn't just rest on the bag any more. This bead is Russian. Anne was wearing a Russian necklace — don't you see — don't you see —"

Miss Silver said, "Yes, I see."

CHAPTER
FOURTEEN

Anne woke up on the following morning with the curious feeling that she had known something in her sleep which had gone from her again. With the light of returning consciousness it had gone, but it had been there. She wondered where things went to when you forgot them. Perhaps it meant that her memory was not gone but was merely sleeping. Perhaps it would come again suddenly and she would remember all those things which she had forgotten.

When Thomasina came in with the tea she lifted a bright face to meet her. Thomasina shook her head.

"There's no cause for you to look as if there was a present for you on the tray," she said.

Anne laughed.

"I feel as if there was, you know." She sat up, snuggling her knees. "Do you believe in presentiments, Thomasina? I'm not sure if I do or not. Tell me, do you ever wake up and feel as if all the bad things had happened and were passed away and done with?"

Thomasina looked at her in a pitying way.

"I can't say I do. And if I did I wouldn't dwell on it, nor yet talk about it."

"Why wouldn't you?"

Thomasina set down the tray.

"Because I wouldn't. And if you'll take my advice you won't do no such thing."

Anne laughed again.

"Why Thomasina — why?"

Thomasina stepped back. Her solid arms hugged one another. She stood and delivered herself.

"Now just you listen to me, my dear. There's times when you wake in the morning and everything looks black to you. No harm in taking a pinch of cheer-me-up those days — no harm at all. But when you wake up and everything's going right and you feel like skipping out of bed and dancing whilst you put your clothes on, that's the time to take a check on yourself and go easy. That's all, my dear. And I'm a quarter of an hour late with the tea through Mattie having forgot to put the kettle on, so I'm all behind — and don't you keep me talking or it'll be the worse for all of us."

Anne laughed again when the door was shut upon Thomasina. The laugh echoed in her head and left a little shiver behind it. She drank her tea and jumped up. The fatigue of the last few days was gone and she felt ready for anything.

She went downstairs, looked out at the day, found it brilliant and beautiful, and began to wonder what she should do with it.

There was sunshine on the lawn. The birches in the distance were golden, and nearer, the clumps of azaleas were crimson and flame-colour. As she stood looking out of the window of the dining-room she thought

74

about gardening — about putting in bulbs. And then suddenly she became aware that that was what she had been used to doing in her old life, the life that was gone. A horrible feeling of loss swept over her. It was just as if she had been at home, and quite suddenly there wasn't a home any more, only this strange place, bare and empty of everything she knew and loved. Past and present rocked together and she felt physically giddy for a moment. Then it was gone again, and she was left wondering, and a little breathless.

When breakfast was over she went out and began on the border again. More and more she found the garden a refuge. It was work she was in the way of doing. Her thoughts went down accustomed paths without effort. Some day she was going to find what she had lost. When she was in the garden she could feel sure of that, and she was content to wait.

It was about an hour after she had gone out that she found her new peace first touched by something alien and discordant. The feeling grew until it became so strong that she turned right round and looked up and down the border to find the cause for it. She had not heard any step, but there, a dozen yards away, was a man watching her.

She rose to her feet instinctively. The man was leaning over the gate which admitted to this part of the garden. He was leaning there, and he was smiling. He had a type of cheap good looks, and his smile was offensive. Her brows drew together as she said, "If you are looking for the house, you have taken the wrong path."

He continued to smile. For a moment she was angry, and then she was frightened. Her heart began to beat violently. She turned pale. She said sharply, "Do you want anything?"

He produced a cigarette and tapped it on his knuckles.

"Ah, now we're getting at it!" he said. There was a trace of an accent. It was no more than a trace. She couldn't tell what it was.

She said, "If you want the house, it's behind you. If you go straight along the path you'll see it."

"How nice that'll be."

He was still smiling, but he didn't move from where he stood leaning over the gate, only he got a box of matches out of his pocket and quite slowly and deliberately he lighted the cigarette. There was something, she didn't know what, that kept her there watching him and waiting for him to speak. It seemed a long time before he did so. When the cigarette was lighted, he took two or three puffs at it before he spoke. Then he said, "You and me've got to have a talk. I gather you wouldn't want to have it in public."

A rushing, dizzying cloud of feeling came over her. She didn't know what she did, or how she looked. When it was gone again, she hadn't moved, but all the blood had left her face. She felt drained and faint. He was speaking, but she had lost what he had said. Only the end of it came to her, faint and thin like something recalled out of the long ago past.

"— never met before —"

She repeated it.

76

"I've never met you before."

He laughed. It was a very unpleasant laugh.

"Is that what you're going to say?"

"It's true."

She hoped with everything in her that it was true.

He drew at his cigarette.

"That's what you say. I might say different. I might say —" He paused, drew on the cigarette again, and let go a long curling trail of smoke. "Oh, well, I take it you know what I might say."

She didn't know. She didn't know a thing. She looked into her own mind, and it was dark. There was nothing there.

He went on just leaning on the gate and smoking with that impudent jaunty stare. She made a great effort.

"I don't know you. I don't know who you are, and I don't want to. Will you please go away."

He took no notice of that at all. He seemed to be considering something in his own mind. In the end he said, "Well, I'll go for now, but you'll please to remember that we know where you are. And there are some orders for you. You'll not tell anyone you've seen me, or what I've said! And when you get your orders you'll do what you're told right away — no niminy piminy nonsense! Do you understand?" He paused, said, "You'd better," and turned round and went away without a single backward look.

When he had gone she went down on her knees by the border and began to turn the earth. She was planting bulbs. The ground had to be cleared for them.

You can't put tulips in on the waste patches of mignonette and snapdragon and the blue, blue flax that looks like sea-water. You can't put anything in on the wrecks of last summer's planting. You must clear the ground for the bulbs, or else they won't grow.

She went on kneeling there, but her hands were idle. The tears were streaming from her eyes. After a time she groped for a handkerchief and dried them. And went on planting the bulbs for the next spring.

CHAPTER
FIFTEEN

Detective Inspector Frank Abbott looked up.

"Well, that's that," he said in a tone of heartfelt satisfaction. He was about to pack up and be off, when a card was brought to him. He looked at it, said "Jim Fancourt —" half to himself, and got to his feet.

"Where is he? Show him in. No, wait a minute — I'll come."

Ten minutes later he was back in his room, with Jim Fancourt saying, "That's about all I can tell you. The last I saw of her was getting on board the plane. And that's all, until I got here and went down to my aunt's house, and there's another girl, a complete and total stranger who has turned up instead of Anne. She's Anne too. What do you make of it?"

"Funny business," said Frank slowly.

Jim nodded.

"This Anne's lost her memory. The first thing she remembers is being on the cellar steps in the dark. She says she was giddy and sat down. There was this bag she speaks of, and when she got over being giddy she picked it up, and there was an electric torch inside."

"Did your Anne have an electric torch?"

"I don't know — I don't think so. I don't know what she had. She came out ready to go with a little bundle of things. I don't know what was in it, but I'm sure she didn't have the bag, because when I gave her ten pounds English money she put it in the front of her dress. She must have got the bag later, after she got home."

"You think it was hers?"

Jim nodded.

"I think so. The other Anne thinks so too. She didn't know anything about it — not about the money or anything. There was about ten pounds left —"

"Go on."

"Well, this is what Anne says. She put on the light, and she saw a dead girl lying at the foot of the steps."

"How does she know she was dead?"

"Head injuries — very extensive. And she was cold. She went down the steps and felt for a pulse. There wasn't any — she's quite clear about that — and she was quite sure the girl was dead. She began to think about getting away. She put out the torch and waited until her sight cleared. Then she came up the steps into the hall of the house. The door was ajar and she let herself out into the street and shut it behind her. Then she walked down the street until she came out on to the main thoroughfare, where she got on a bus. Two streets along Miss Silver got on to the same bus."

Frank cocked an eyebrow.

"Miss Silver?"

"Miss Maud Silver. She noticed the girl. She got out with her at Victoria and spoke to her. She gave her tea, and she got in return this extraordinary story."

"And what does Miss Silver say to it?"

"Miss Silver thinks it's true. By the time they'd had tea together she had made up her mind and told Anne what to do. She was to go down to Haleycott to my aunts and wait till I arrived, or till her memory came back. I got in this morning and went down there. My aunts are" — he made a face — "well, they're old-maidish."

Frank held up a hand.

"Wait a minute," he said, "you're going too fast. You haven't said how she knew where to go."

Jim bit his lip.

"Sorry," he said. "I keep thinking I've told you more than I have. I did say she'd got a bag, didn't I — the bag the money was in and the torch? Well, there was a letter in it too from my aunt Lilian, inviting her down there. You see, I'd written to her. They're old-fashioned, she and Harriet — lived at Haleycott all their lives, or most of them — and I thought it best to give them a little warning, so I sent Anne to this Mrs Birdstock, an old parlourmaid of ours. She was to post the letter I had written to Lilian as soon as she arrived and wait with Mrs Birdstock for an answer. Well, she didn't do any of those things. That is, she must have sent my letter to Lilian, because the answer to it came there to Saltcoats Road. But she didn't go there, and she didn't wait there. I don't know where she went or what she did. And someone — someone turned up on the third day at Saltcoats Road, said she was Anne, and took away the letter from Lilian. It may have been Anne, or it may have been someone else. If it was *Anne*, it's the

81

last time she appeared alive as far as we know. There's one thing, the bag Anne — the Anne who is alive, not the poor girl who was dead in the cellar — the bag that had the money in it . . . No, I'm getting this all wrong, and it'll fog you. Wait a minute. Anne — the living Anne, the girl who is down at Haleycott now — when she turned up in the bus and Miss Silver met her, she had a handbag. It's the first appearance of a handbag, so it's important. Anne, the one who's alive, doesn't think that the bag belongs to her.

"She thinks it belonged to the dead girl. I think it was one of the things she bought when she landed. She had very little with her — I don't know what she had, but she didn't have a bag."

"You don't know that the bag didn't belong to the other girl?"

"Well, I don't know anything — but I'm guessing. It seems reasonable the way I'm telling it."

"Look here, what actually was there in that bag?"

"A handkerchief, a letter from my aunt Lilian, notes to the amount of ten pounds in the middle, and a little change in the small purse at the side. There was a torch. Anne said she got it out and looked at the dead girl, then she put it away again. That's the lot."

Frank was silent for a moment. Then he said, "And you found this bead in the cellar of a house in Lime Street?"

"Yes — 37 Lime Street."

"And you're sure that bead you found is from the girl's necklace?"

Jim said, "Look here, I'm not sure about anything. If we were in Russia, there wouldn't be anything to be sure about — every second girl might be wearing a necklace of that sort. As we're in London —" He made a gesture with his hands. "It tots up, doesn't it? There's this Russian bead on the floor of an empty house, just out of sight — doesn't that say anything to you? And the floor had been swept and washed as far as the boards leaning up against the wall in the corner. I tell you the girl was murdered there, and I want to know who murdered her. And why."

CHAPTER
SIXTEEN

Jim came down to Chantreys the following morning. He was received by Harriet with indifference, by Lilian with an intensification of her usual somewhat fluttered and inconsequent manner.

Left alone with Anne for a moment, he said in a low voice, "I want to talk to you. Get your hat on and come out."

When Lilian reappeared he said, "We're going out."

Lilian said, "Oh?" and then quickly, "Well, it's not very convenient, not at all convenient, but if you want — only after lunch would be much better."

"I shan't be here after lunch. I've just come down for an hour to see Anne. It is Anne and I who are going out."

"Oh?" Lilian looked cross and offended. "Of course, if that is what you want you must do just as you like."

He turned to Anne.

"Put on your things and come along, will you?"

Lilian said in a quick waspish way, "You're very sure of who you want, aren't you? You're very sure about everything."

Anne hurried to be gone. She heard Jim's voice behind her as she went, but she couldn't hear what he said. She fetched a scarf and her coat, and came back to find Lilian writing and Jim looking out of the window. There was a heavy feeling in the air as if there had been a quarrel between them. At the sound of her light footstep he turned and went out with her, up through the garden and out through a low wicket gate upon the green empty slopes of the hill.

They had not spoken until they were clear of the garden. Then he turned to her and said, "This is a first-class place for confidences. Ideal. I don't like doors and walls very much. And I don't like bushes and trees where you can't see — there may be nothing, or there may be anything. The best place for talking secrets is a mountain top with no trees, or a boat on the sea without anyone to overhear what you are saying. But this is good enough."

If he had been a little uncertain about Anne, her presence was convincing. She had walked beside him in a silence which was without constraint. It was most like the silence of intimacy, the silence into which two old friends may fall when they walk together. There was a restful quiet about it. She did not answer him now, only waited, looking not at him but at the slopes of bare green turning rusty, and at the trees which surrounded the house which they had left. He had not been able to make up his mind what to say to her, and then all at once his mind was made up, set, and fixed. What he knew she could know — it was as simple and as easy as that. He said, "I went to see Miss Silver yesterday."

"Yes?"

It was just one word, but he knew when he heard it that that was how it was to be between them.

"We found the house —"

She said "Oh —" It was more a breath than a word.

"The floor of the cellar had been swept and washed, but in the corner there were some boards. They hadn't been moved. I moved them. This was lying underneath them." He held out his palm with the bead upon it — a small blue bead — evidence of murder —

She met his eyes. Something seemed to pass between them. She said very low, "Her beads were like that."

"You saw them?"

"Yes. They had been — round her neck. The string was broken —" She was looking back into the dark cellar. The light came from the torch in her hand, the light dazzled on the beads. She said, "I saw them there in the cellar — I did see them —"

He spoke insistently.

"You're sure you saw them — the beads?"

"Yes, I'm sure." A shudder shook her. "They were there — the beads — but the string was broken —"

He said, "We were there — Miss Silver and I. The house is to let furnished. The old lady it belonged to died. Which way did you go down to the cellar from the hall — right or left?"

"I don't know." She shook her head. And then it came to her. "I don't know about going down — but coming up — the door was on my right. There was the flight of steps — and then the door — it was half open — but no light in the hall. There was a table between me and the outside door — I had to go round it — the door was a little open. I went out and shut the door behind me. It was a dark road, but there were a lot of lights at the far end of it. I went along to the lights. I got into the first bus that stopped."

He was frowning intently.

"You don't remember going to the house — who let you in?"

She shook her head.

"I don't remember anything like that —" She paused. "If I had seen anyone — anyone at all — wouldn't I remember them?"

"I don't know."

"I think I should. I don't think I saw anyone in that house. I think we were alone there — the dead girl and myself. I don't think there was anyone else. If there was, why didn't they come and kill me too? I think the house was empty."

He thought so too, but he said nothing. It was a moment before he spoke.

"How many steps were there from the ground floor of the cellar to the hall?"

All this time she had been looking at him. Now her expression altered. She shut her eyes, and her lips moved. It came to him that she was counting the steps. She was back in the cellar, sitting on the steps with the torch in her hand and the faintness passing away. Six steps down — and the floor — and the girl's body — lying there — dead — six steps down. How many steps up from where she had been sitting, trying to control fear — the horror of being alone with the dead? There were more steps above her than below.

She opened her eyes, met his, and said, "It was six steps down from where I was — and six or seven steps up — I can't tell exactly."

He said, "That's near enough."

There was a long pause between them. She had the feeling of having given out all she had to give. It left her drained and weak. He said suddenly, "You'd never seen the girl before?"

"No, never. At least I don't think so — I don't remember."

He was frowning again.

"How on earth did you get mixed up in it?"

"I don't know — I can't remember." Then she made a small movement towards him. "Something happened yesterday."

"What?"

"There was a man — I was planting bulbs — I looked up, and he was where that gate opens on the border, leaning on it, smoking."

"Yes?"

"I thought — he had mistaken his way. He stood there — smiling. He lighted a cigarette. Then he said —" It swept over her again, the dreadful feeling which she had had in that man's presence. Everything darkened. She put out her hand and Jim took it. It was only then that she felt how icy cold she was — how cold. His hands were warm. Their warmth brought her consciousness back.

He saw her turn fainting white. And then he saw the colour come again to her lips, to her cheek. He had a quite extraordinary sensation of having come home. He said, "Anne — Anne — you're safe — you're home. Don't — Anne — darling!"

For a moment she leaned against him. Then she said in a confused sort of way, "I'm so sorry — I didn't mean to. Oh, I'm stupid!" Her eyes were full of tears. She groped in her pocket for her handkerchief and dried them, leaning against him. Then she said, "I don't know what made me do that. He — he frightened me — I don't know why."

"He frightened you? What did he say?"

"He said we'd got to have a talk. He said I wouldn't want to have it in public. I — I turned faint like I did just now — I don't know why. It frightened me — he frightened me. I said I had never met him before, and he laughed. He — he stood there and smoked. He said I knew what he might say —" Her voice went away to a whisper on the word. "But I didn't — I didn't — oh, I didn't. I didn't know anything. I think that's what frightened me. If I could have remembered, no matter what it was, I wouldn't have been so frightened. It's not knowing — not being able to see. It's like waking up in the night and not knowing where you are."

His arm was round her again. She leaned against him and trembled. He said, "Go on."

"There wasn't much more. I said I didn't know him — I didn't know who he was, I didn't want to. I said would he please go away. And he said —" Her colour all went again and she gripped his arm, but her voice came steadily. "He said, 'Well, I'll go for now. Remember, we know where you are.' Then he said he'd got some orders for me. I wasn't to tell anyone I'd seen him or what he had said, and when I got my orders I was to do just what I was told — at once. He said, 'You'd better!' and he turned round and went away." She paused for a moment, and then she said, speaking very low and in a piteous hurried manner, "I don't know what he meant, but it frightened me — dreadfully."

He considered that, holding her hand in a strong tight clasp, only half aware of what he was doing or of the fact that what would have hurt her at a time of full security was in her present state something which she would not be without. In the end he spoke.

"You don't remember him?"

"No — not at all. I don't believe I had ever seen him before."

"Then why should he speak to you like that?"

"I don't know. I really don't."

He looked at her with the same frowning gaze. When she had seen it before it had set her wondering what she had said or done to anger him. Now in a strange sort of way she knew the frown for what it was, a deep concern for her, a deepening interest.

He said abruptly, "Listen to me! I don't like leaving you here, but I don't see any way out of it — not at present. All the same I don't like it very much, but you should be all right if you do just what I say. Now listen! You're not to go out of sight of another person — old Clarke in the garden — one of the people in the house. You're not to go out by yourself — do you hear?"

"Yes, I hear, but —"

90

"There isn't any but. You do what you're told, and you'll be safe!" He repeated the word. "Safe. That's what you want to be, isn't it? And at present I can't protect you because I don't know enough. I've got to find out who you are, how you come into this business, how to make you safe. And you've got to help. You can do that in two ways. You can do just what I say — never be out of sight of someone you can call to for help. And if you remember anything — anything at all — ring me up and tell me what it is. I think your memory will come back. Don't strain, don't try to remember. That's not the way. But if you do remember anything, ring me up at once. Here's an address that will find me within an hour or two." He let go of her hand and wrote on a leaf torn from a scrubby notebook. "These people will know where I am and what I am doing. You can speak freely to them."

"To anyone who answers the telephone?"

"Yes. And there'll be someone there always. It's this end you'll have to look out for. Don't talk to anyone here. Lilian's all right, but she's a fool. And Harriet — oh, they're all right, but they haven't as much sense as you could put on a three-penny bit. So you won't tell them anything — nothing at all! Is that understood?"

She said, "Yes." It was more than an agreement. It was a promise, and he took it as such.

He said, "All right. Then we'll be getting back. I haven't too much time."

She didn't say it aloud, but it came up in her with a kind of shaking strength.

"Too much time — no, there isn't too much time at all."

Afterwards she was to wish that she had said it to him.

CHAPTER
SEVENTEEN

It seemed no time at all until he was gone. The day went by and the night came. She went up to bed early. There was a kind of hush upon her spirits. Looking back on it afterwards, it seemed strange to her. It was as if everything waited, she didn't know for what. She only knew that there was nothing she could do about it — nothing except wait. Deep in her mind the question asked itself, "What am I waiting for?" and every time that happened something moved quickly in those under places and shut it away.

By the time that coffee had been drunk and the tray removed she was so tired that sleeping and waking seemed to be part of a pattern in which she moved uncertainly, with now one side of her awake and on the point of knowing what there was to be known about herself, about the dead girl, about the man who had threatened her; and now another side, not seen but dimly felt, pressing in, just not realized, but certain, sure, and inevitable. Except momentarily, there was no fear. She was able to talk.

There was a long period during which Lilian talked interminably about Christmas cards — how they must be certain to go over the list thoroughly and cut them down as much as possible.

"Because really they are at least three times as expensive as they used to be, and though I don't grudge anything to anyone, I must say it does seem a *waste*, because anything that is worthwhile spending on at all is such a price that I'm sure I don't know where people get the money from."

Harriet looked up and said, "If nobody sent any cards, we shouldn't have them for the hospital. It's dreadful to think of people throwing them away, when you think what has been spent on them."

Lilian gave a sharp little glance at Anne.

"I suppose you won't have any cards to send," she said.

Anne wondered what she was to say to that. Then she found herself saying, "No."

"It gets worse and worse," said Lilian. "Every year."

Harriet put down her coffee-cup.

"Well, we needn't think about it yet," she said.

For some reason the phrase went in and out of Anne's shifting thought. No need to think or plan for Christmas or any other future day. Take things as they come. Take things as they are. What does it matter? There's one end to everything.

Then suddenly she was broad awake. The soothing, loving tides, the half-consciousness, slid away and she was broad awake — broad awake and just about to see what it all meant. It was something she didn't want to see. It was something horrible and frightening. And then suddenly, just as she was going to see what it was, it was gone again and the mists closed down. Her mind was full of mist. The room seemed to swirl. She didn't know where she was for a moment. She didn't know that all the colour had left her face, and that she was staring blankly. And then after a moment the room cleared again. She saw the heavy old-fashioned curtains drawn across the windows, the clutter of furniture, the brass tray with the coffee-cups which someone had brought from India fifty or sixty years ago, the tall cupboards full of china, the sofa and the chairs, the carpet with its wreaths of flowers all gone away to a dull drab, and Lilian, sitting there looking at her.

Harriet was reading a heavy book. She wasn't watching them. But Lilian, Lilian was looking at her with the strangest expression. A little picture came up in Anne's mind — the picture of a cat waiting by a mouse-hole. Lilian was looking at her like that. She made a very great effort and pushed the picture away. Her thoughts cleared.

Lilian said, "Are you tired?"

"Yes, I'm tired — I don't know why."

"You had better go off to bed early. Harriet often goes early. I sit up to all hours, so don't wait for me."

She waited till Thomasina came for the tray, and then said good-night and went upstairs to bed.

Sleep came down on her like a rushing black cloud. Afterwards, when she thought about it, she was to wonder about that sleep. Was it just that she was tired, that she had been under a strain? Or was there another reason for that rushing down of the curtain of darkness? She was never to be quite sure, but her movements grew slower and slower, and the last thing she remembered was blowing out the candle by her bed. Nothing after that at all — nothing but the direct and distinct sensation of seeing the candle-flame very large and bright, a large bright flame to be blown at. She could remember blowing at it, and then darkness succeeded light and she couldn't remember anything more at all, only a black unconsciousness that pressed in upon her and contained no living thought. It wasn't like sleep. Sleep was natural and refreshing. This unconsciousness was like being drowned fathoms deep. When you were asleep you rested. Now she didn't rest at all. There was a struggle going on. She struggled to come back out of the darkness, out of the horrible pit, and she couldn't — she couldn't. The darkness came in waves; it rose against her and flowed in. Then she would struggle against the blackness, against suffocation, against the imminent deadly knowledge which lay behind the blackness. Every time she got to that, to the fact that there was some knowledge which eluded her, she went down again into the blackness and the confusion.

And then suddenly the dream broke and she was free. She lay on her back with her arms stretched out, and she was panting and sobbing, "No — no — no —!" And all the time the blessed waking world came in on her thought and became the real.

She sat up in bed panting. She had had a horrible dream. She didn't know what it was, but it had been there and it was gone again. Thank God it was gone. She got out of bed. No watch or clock in the room, and

96

she had no idea of the time. She went to the window and opened it. She never slept with her window shut. That was it of course. She hadn't opened the window. She had been too sleepy to open it. She had had a horrible nightmare. She leaned right out and let the cool air flow over her. Her throat was dry and her head felt hot. It was a still, calm night. She thought of water, running and bubbling and very, very cold, and from there her thoughts turned to a long cool drink.

She drew back from the window, and the room felt very dark. Outside the night was clear. You could see the curve of the drive, the trees, the black tracery, and the clear depths of the sky. To turn from them was like turning from sight to blindness. Fear touched her again, a light shiver went over her. And then she was wide awake, tingling with a sudden imminent thought. If it was so late, if so much time had gone by, why was there light on the other side of her door? She didn't knew why the question frightened her so much. She only knew that it did frighten her. And then quite suddenly as she looked at it the streak of light under her door disappeared. It went out and left her looking at darkness.

After a little the faint, pale outdoor shine was free again. She remained standing quite still for some minutes. Then she began to count steadily and monotonously. When she had got up to five hundred she stopped and listened again. There was no sound. There was no sound at all. She drew a long breath. Two voices warred in her. One of them said, "What nonsense! You wake up and there's a light in the passage — what about it? You don't even know what time it is." The other voice said, "I could find out." Then the first voice again, "You daren't. You daren't put on a light to look. Suppose there's someone waiting in the dark just to see if you do anything at all."

A deep sharp pang of terror went through her. It was true what the voice said — she didn't dare. And she knew with a dreadful passionate certainty that what she did now in the next few minutes would have power over her for the rest of her life. She thought of Jim. He wouldn't let anything hurt her. He didn't believe that there was anything to hurt her here, or he wouldn't have gone away and left her to it. And then she knew that it was no use thinking of Jim, because he wasn't here. She had to depend on herself. She went to the door and opened it.

The darkness outside was absolute. She stood there listening. There was no sound. Her room opened upon a cross passage. At the end of the passage there was a landing, and the stair going down. She went barefoot along the passage to the landing and leaned over the rail that ran along it.

A small light burned in the hall below. She tried to think whether it burned there all night. Perhaps it did. Perhaps she had imagined the light she had seen under the door in her room. Perhaps she had dreamed about it. Perhaps she was dreaming now. She shuddered violently and turned back.

It was quite dark in the passage. She felt her way along it to the open door of her room. Her coat — she must put on her coat. She went to the wardrobe and opened it. It felt like a black cavern, and it was empty except for her coat, and her shirt and skirt. At that moment, curiously and blindingly, she remembered that she had a red dress — dark red. It was her best dress. She wondered where it was now. She wondered if she would ever see it again. And then her groping hands were on the collar of a coat and she unhooked it and slipped it on.

It was warm. She had not known that she was cold until she put it on. Nothing made you so cold as fear. She was very much afraid. She turned round from the wardrobe and made her way across the room to the door. And out of the door into the length of dark passage and along it to the landing.

On the landing itself she stopped. Darkness covered you. Darkness was safe. She couldn't come out of its protection into the light and down the stairs and across the hall. She couldn't — she couldn't. The very thought of it made her limbs shake and brought the taste of fear up into her throat.

And then suddenly she thought about the back stairs. That was it. She would only have to cross this wide shadowy passage to the other side of the house, and the quicker she did it the better. Every moment that she stood and waited, the little courage that she had would be draining away. She mustn't wait — she mustn't wait at all. It was quite easy, there was no danger. Her heart banged against her side and she did it. Now she was across the dimly lighted space, and now the black mouth of the passage was open before her.

Every step she took away from the light made her safer. In her dark coat she couldn't really be seen now. No one would look this way. The back stair went down two-thirds of the way along the passage. It was screened by a door. Sometimes the door stood open. Mattie was careless about leaving it. If Thomasina had come up last, it would be shut. It was open. Walking in the dark with what light there was getting fainter and fainter behind her, she came upon it, her fingers feeling along the wall. And then quite suddenly the edge of the door, and then nothing. The door was open, and there was no light — no light at all.

She slipped into the darkness, shut the door, and took a long breath. She did not know how frightened she had been until it was over. Now she stood for a moment, pulling herself together.

It was quite, quite dark. After a moment or two she began to move her foot half a step at a time. She thought there was a sort of landing there, taps and a sink on one side, and steps going down on the other. She had to be very careful. If she made a false step, anyone might hear her. She took two steps — three, with her hand before her — four — five — and then there was the stair-rail, and her foot poised over nothingness. Her hand touched the rail just in time to prevent a loss of balance. She gripped hard on the rail and went down. She wasn't quite sure where the stair came out.

When she had reached the last of the steps she had to feel about her. There was another door, shut this time. She opened it and found herself in a dark

100

passage. At that moment there came over her a desperate longing to be back in her room warm in her bed. It came and it went again. Afterwards she thought that was the last moment at which she could have drawn back. It was her opportunity, and she refused it. From then on she had no choice.

CHAPTER
EIGHTEEN

In the study Lilian Fancourt sat bolt upright on the sofa. Her expression was strained, her face very white. She was looking at the man who sat beside her, his whole appearance that of someone who is quite sure of himself. He said in an easy manner, "Come along, Lilian — what's all the fuss about? I'm not going to eat her."

Lilian brightened a little. She said, "N-no —"

He laughed.

"Anyone would think I was asking you to do something dreadful, my dear."

"Oh, you're not — are you?"

"Of course I'm not. I'm only asking you to help me to restore a poor lost girl to her nearest relation. You've really no truck with her at all, you know. She's not married to your nephew and never has been, and if I take her off in the middle of the night, well, she's run away and that's all there is to it. Next time she turns up, if she turns up at all, it'll be as a blushing bride."

Lilian gave him a curious frightened look.

"What do you mean?"

"What I've said."

"What do you mean by saying 'if she turns up at all'?"

"Oh, just a manner of speaking."

"You wouldn't hurt her — you don't mean that!"

He laughed.

"Look here, my dear, she's got money, and if she was out of the way it would all go to Charity with a nice big C. You've known me a good long time. Have I ever struck you as being the sort of chump who would go out of his way to endow a charity?"

"N-no — you haven't." Lilian looked at him out of the corners of her eyes. It was curious to see him after — how long was it — fifteen years? No, it must be near twenty — but it might have been yesterday. She let her thoughts run back. He had always taken the high hand . . . She wouldn't really have liked it. She and Harriet were better off as they were. And yet — and yet —

His voice cut in.

"My dear girl, what's all the fuss about?"

CHAPTER
NINETEEN

Anne went on through the door into the hall. The light seemed frighteningly bright to her eyes which had accustomed themselves to the darkness. She had come out into the back part of the hall. What light there was came from the single jet turned low just inside the hall door. The first door on her right led into the dining-room, and beyond it, to the front of the house, was the room where they had sat after dinner. It was the room where Lilian had her writing-table. Light shone under the door. Straining, she thought she could catch the sound of voices. She stood still and listened. The murmur of voices went on.

And then she had a sudden fright. One of the voices rose, came nearer. She darted for the dining-room door. It was level with her. She was inside and the door held close in front of her — not shut but just held close. She stood there, her heart beating so loud that it seemed to her that anyone would be able to hear it and follow the sound and find her.

Moments passed. Her heart-beats quieted. And then when she could hear again there was sound coming, not through the door whose handle she clutched, but from behind her. She turned round. The door against which she had been leaning, the door into the hall, wasn't shut. But the sound didn't come from there. It came from in front of her on the right-hand side. It came from the next-door room, and she remembered that there was a door between the two rooms.

When the house was built all those years ago, when old Mr Fancourt was young, there had been gay parties in the house and provision made for guests to circulate. Lilian's voice, explaining that of course they lived very differently now since the two wars, came to her.

"Of course, we don't remember its gay days. He wasn't so young when he married our mother." Lilian's high, affected voice came trailing out of her memory as she crossed the dark dining-room step by cautious step. She mustn't make any noise at all or they would hear her as she could hear them.

She was about half-way across the room, her hands feeling before her and the carpet soft under her feet, when it came to her with paralysing suddenness that one of the people she could hear speaking next door was a man. It came to her with terrifying suddenness. From that moment when her own heart had quieted and she had really begun to listen, it had been Lilian's voice to which she had been listening. And then suddenly there was a man speaking. It was strange to her, and yet not strange at all. It wasn't Jim's voice. Quite definitely it wasn't his.

She went on moving slowly and carefully until she came to the door between the two rooms. Her hands groping in front of her felt the panels of the door. They came flat against it and stayed there. Her forehead came down between them and was pressed against the dark panel. She heard the man say, "You'd much better leave it all to me," and in that moment she knew that the man who was speaking was the man who had watched her in the garden. She had been on her knees planting the bulbs, and she had looked up and seen him. It swept out of her memory and caught her back. It took her a moment to shake it off and to come again to the dark room with her hands pressed against the door and her forehead leaning against it. It took her a moment to be where she was, not where she had been.

She came back and listened to the voices on the other side of the dark door. She must have missed something, because what she heard was Lilian again — not what she said, but her voice leaving off as if she had been speaking and then had stopped. And quite clear on that again, the man's voice, a little louder.

"Dry up, will you! The less you know about this the better! You do what you're told and that's all you've got to bother about!"

"I don't think —"

"You don't need to think! You do just what you're told and no harm will come to you! You start thinking, and before you know where you are you'll be in difficulties! And if you get into difficulties, you can get out of them all on your own as far as I'm concerned!"

Then Lilian again.

"Oh, no, I didn't mean that. I wish you wouldn't — you confuse me so — I only meant —"

He said, "Dry up! You'd better! When I want you to think or plan anything I'll let you know! Which room is she in?"

"Upstairs. But I don't think —"

"Dry up! I'll take her now — no time like the present. She's been here long enough — too long. If I'd thought for a moment . . . Now, look here —"

Anne seemed to come to herself. She had this minute — only this minute. It didn't matter what they said, or what they were going to say, she had just this minute in which to save herself. Her hands, which were flat on the door, pushed her back from it. It was as if they had a life and energy of their own. They pushed her, and she was upright. And then the same curious force seemed to turn her and she retraced her steps. There was just one moment when she stopped. She was half-way to the door, and the man laughed. Everything in her went cold at the sound. She stopped and stood with her bare feet on the thick, warm carpet and felt the deadly cold pass over her. She did not know that the laugh might have driven her into headlong flight. If it had done that, nothing could have saved her. It was the age-old instinct to be still, not to move, that had saved her. She stood and waited. When her pulses had died down she moved on towards the door.

It was terrible to leave the dark room for the lighted hall. It was harder now than it had been. The thought went through her mind that if it was so hard as not to be possible she was lost. The fear of that struck into her and took her across the strip of lighted hall between the doorway of the dining-room and the door which led to the safe back stair.

When she was in the dark again, the terror that was upon her slackened a little. She came out upon the cross passage which ran through the house and made her way along it to the landing, and so back again to her room.

The room felt safe, but it wasn't. Nothing under this roof was safe. Nothing at all. She began to dress herself. The clothes she put on struck cold against her. She felt in the cupboard and found her coat and skirt and the shirt which went with it. She must be quick — oh, she must be quick. And she didn't dare to make a light, she didn't dare. She put on her shoes and stockings, and the shirt, and the coat and skirt, the hat, and the top coat, and she was at the door.

The passage was dark and empty. Just one more effort and she would be free. A tune and the fragment of a song came into her mind as she stood there looking out at the dark passage brightening towards the landing, darkening again on the other side.

One more river and that's the river of Jordan,
One more river, one more river to cross.

Suddenly she felt quick, and clear, and calm. She was going to get away, and nobody was going to stop her.

She went quietly along the brightening way, across the landing, and made her way along the passage to the stair down which she had gone before.

108

CHAPTER
TWENTY

When the back door shut behind her all her pulses leapt. She stood for a moment, hardly able to draw breath, hardly able to think. And then her hand let go of the door-handle. She was out. She was free. She could go away and never come back again.

She began to move, to get away from the house. She wasn't safe here — so near. And she must go carefully. No tripping over anything, no noise. She must take her time, step by step, step by cautious step. No use thinking what she was going to do. What she had to do now was to get away, to get as far as she could from the man, and from Lilian. She must keep her mind steadily on getting away.

The most dangerous part was the immediate part. She had to skirt the house and come out into the drive. She was on the path to the back door, the path on the east side of the house. Every day she had seen tradespeople come in and go round to the back. It was a driving road but a narrow one. There was a space to turn in behind the ornamental screen of cypress and rhododendron which hid the back door. If she followed this driving road it would bring her out on to the main road. She went on until she was clear of the yard, until her breath came easier, until she believed that she was really going to get away.

The back way out lay before her. She could go a little faster now, but not too fast. She came in herself, on the dreadful possibility that if she ran she might lose control. She had a terrible quick picture of herself running and screaming — screaming — She stood quite still and fought down the thing that wanted to run and scream. When it was under lock and key, she began to walk again. She did not dare to run.

She began to think what she must do. There were the trains, but she did not know when the last one went. And what would she do when she reached the other end? She didn't know whether you were allowed to stop in the station. She didn't even know if it would be safe to stop. Nothing was safe any more, even now, even here. Nothing was safe. She had a little time in hand and no more — just a little time whilst Lilian and the man sat talking — before they discovered that she had run away. She had a curious moment when she saw this time as a handful of jewels, bright and glistening. She had them, and she had nothing more at all. If she did not make good use of them they would dissolve and melt away and be utterly gone. They would not keep. She must use them now.

There was a sound in her ears. It was the sound of a car coming up behind her. It startled her broad awake out of her fancies and her dreams. She didn't know where it came from, or where it was going to. It went past her, going very fast and with no thought of her at all. She stood for a moment and watched it go.

110

Gradually the sound of it died away. The bright light was gone and she was all alone in the dark again. She began to run towards the station.

She didn't know when it came to her, but it stopped her dead. One minute she was running with only one thought in her mind, to reach light, people, the station, and then all of a sudden she was standing still, checked as if by a wall. There wasn't any wall, there wasn't anything to stop her going on to the station except the fact that it was no good going on, because there wouldn't be any train until 6.20 in the morning. It was Thomasina who had mentioned the 6.20 only yesterday, and she had laughed and said, "How frightfully early!" But it wasn't early enough — it wasn't nearly early enough. It must be about twelve o'clock — perhaps half-past twelve. Six hours before any train would leave the station. What was she to do? She stood quite still and shuddered. But it wouldn't do to stand still. At any moment they might find out that she had run away, and he would come after her. She made a great effort and looked about her.

The night was not dark. A little fitful moonlight and some cloud that veiled it from time to time. There was a house not very far away. She tried to think whose it could be. The house lay on the right of the road. On the left there were open fields with no hedge to screen her. If the man came down the road in a car looking for her he would see her on the field side. No use getting in there. She turned to the house. Suppose she were to knock them up — tell them the truth. She said, "I can't," and was swamped by the unbelievable story she

111

would have to tell. And he, the man — he would only have to say she was his niece, his sister, and she had lost her memory and given them all a terrible fright. She didn't even know his name. He could make up anything he liked about her, he could put up a tale that anyone would believe, and she hadn't so much as the shred of a fact to bring against him.

If she could only get to Miss Silver — if she could get to Jim. And then like a dizzying blow the thought struck her. Jim — wasn't he in this? Lilian was. Something pulled at her heart. If Jim was in on this betrayal, she might as well give up. And then, quick on that, she found herself defending him. He wasn't in on it — he couldn't be. There were reasons why he couldn't be. She would think of them presently. Not now — it didn't matter now. What mattered at the present moment was that she should get off the road before anyone found her there.

She went to the right and climbed up half a dozen steps to the front door of the house that stood there, and as she did so a car came up the road behind her, going slowly.

CHAPTER
TWENTY-ONE

Jim Fancourt went to Scotland Yard as soon as he got up to town. He walked in on Frank Abbott, who was writing, and said with hardly a preliminary, "She doesn't know anything."

Frank laid down his pen and lifted his eyebrows.

"She?" he said.

Jim frowned.

"Anne — the other girl — the one who found her dead. I told you all about it."

Frank's brows went a little higher.

"*All?*" he said.

"All I knew. I've got a little more, but not much."

"What have you got?"

"I went down and saw Anne. She identified the bead I showed you. It was one of a string round Anne Borrowdale's neck. She said the string was broken. She says she saw the beads there in the cellar — she did see them. I told her about going to the house with Miss Silver, and it all fits. She doesn't remember going down to the cellar. Her recollection begins half-way down the stairs like I told you. She went down, and made sure that the girl she saw was dead. I told you all that, didn't

I? And when she was sure, she wanted to get away, and I don't blame her. Do you?"

"No."

"When she was sure the girl was dead she put out the torch and came up the stairs. I told you about all that — her walking along the street, and getting on the bus, and meeting Miss Silver. Well, I went down yesterday and saw her. I told her that I'd been to look for the house, and I showed her the bead. She turned awfully pale when she saw it, and she said the beads that had been round the girl's neck were like that. I pressed her, and she stuck to it. She said she was sure she had seen them. She shuddered violently when she said it — it evidently brought the whole thing back. She said, 'They were there — but the string was broken!' I pressed her about going to the house. She couldn't remember anything — anything at all — before the moment when she found herself on the cellar stairs with the consciousness that something dreadful had happened. It was after that that she sat down on the steps and waited for her head to clear. She found the bag, got out the torch, and saw the dead girl at the foot of the steps." He made an impatient gesture. "I told you all that! What's the good of going over and over it! But it was then that she saw the beads that had been round the girl's neck. And the string was broken — this one had rolled away and got behind some boards that were leaning up against the wall. Everything else had been cleaned up — washed — tidied away. There was just this one bead behind the boards, and it proves the whole story, doesn't it?"

"Well — we'd like to see the girl. Anything more?"

Jim frowned.

"No — not really. She says that she thinks the house was empty when she was in it."

"Why?"

"She says why didn't they kill her too if they were there?"

"How did she get into the house?"

"She doesn't know. Everything's a blank up to the moment she came to in the dark on those steps —" He paused, and then said, "I think she'd seen the dead girl and dropped her own torch — she thinks she had a torch. There was a broken one on the ground by the dead girl. The one she used afterwards was in the bag — the black bag which she thinks must have belonged to the dead Anne. It was lying on the steps beside her. She put out her hand and felt it there when she was sitting down and trying not to faint. She picked it up and opened it, and there was a torch inside, besides some loose change and ten pounds in notes in the inside pocket. I told you all that. She says she doesn't think the bag was hers, or the money, or the torch. As far as she is concerned she starts from scratch — there on the cellar steps without a penny."

Frank Abbott frowned.

"Give me her description."

"Whose — the dead Anne's, or the living?"

"Both."

Jim said, "This Anne, the living one, she's tall and slim. She's anything between twenty and twenty-five —

115

I should say nearer twenty — say twenty-two, twenty-three. Brown hair — dark brown — curly —"

Frank Abbott said, "That's nothing to go by. Very few girls let themselves have straight hair nowadays. Any distinguishing marks?"

"No. How do you suppose I should know? There aren't any that show."

"And the dead girl?"

Jim stared at him.

"What's the good of describing anyone? What's the good of a description? The dead Anne was a little thicker set and not so tall — about the same age. She had curly hair — it would be naturally curly, I should think, because there wouldn't be permanent-waving machines out where we were, and she'd been there more than a year with her father."

Frank Abbott looked up sharply and said, "Were you married to her — this girl who is dead?"

"Not really — there was some kind of a ceremony."

Frank's hand lifted and fell again.

"You told the Americans that she was your wife."

"Only way I could get them to take her."

Frank remarked dispassionately, "There'll be a row about that."

"Can't be helped. If she'd been alive — but she isn't, poor girl, she's dead. It's the other one, the living Anne, who's got to be considered now. There's something going on, I don't know what, but yesterday a man turned up to see her. I've just come up from there, and she told me about it. Now listen — this is what she said. She was planting bulbs, and he came up the

116

garden by himself. She thought he had mistaken the way. When she was telling me about it she was frightened — so frightened that she nearly fainted. We were out on the hillside above the house. I took her out there because I didn't want anyone eavesdropping." He paused.

Frank said, "Go on."

"I said, 'He's frightened you — what did he say?' And she said —" He paused.

For a moment he was back on the hillside. He was alone with Anne and she was speaking — "*He said we've got to have a talk, and I wouldn't want to have it in public. I — I turned faint like I did just now, I don't know why.*" He came back to the office with the voice dying away in his ears — "*It frightened me — it frightened me —*"

Frank was looking at him. Jim went on speaking. He repeated her words, the description of the man, and his last words.

"He said, 'I'll go for now. You'll remember that we know where you are. And here are some orders for you. You'll not tell anyone you've seen me, or what I've said. And when you get your orders you'll do what you're told right away, and no nonsense about it! Do you understand?' Then he said, 'You'd better!' and he went away. And that was all."

Frank Abbott said, "Very peremptory."

Jim frowned and said, "Yes."

CHAPTER
TWENTY-TWO

Anne's heart fainted in her. He had caught her. She put her hand on the handle of the door to steady herself. And it turned. It wasn't a locked door barring her way to safety. It was open, and she was safe. The door swung in, and she with it. She shut it behind her, locked it, and leaned against it in the darkness. She felt faint with the narrowness of her escape. And then from the back of the hall in which she was standing a door opened and light shone out. A voice which was young, quite young, said sleepily, "Is that you? How late you are!"

There was a girl, and she was yawning. Behind her there was a partly open door to a lighted room. The light was dangerous. It was the dead middle of the night. There oughtn't to be any light in a sleeping house. She moved so quickly that she had no time for anything except that one thought. The darkness was safe, the light was dangerous. She was along the passage and at the door, and in the same moment she was in the room and the door shut on her and on the girl. She leaned against it, drawing quick breaths and saying the first thing that came into her mind to say.

"I'm so sorry. There's a man — chasing me. Oh, please do help me!"

The girl looked at her. She was a little thing, and plump. Her fair hair was untidy, as if she had been asleep on it. She had on a short skirt and a flannel blouse, and she had kicked off her shoes. They were lying higgledy piggledy in front of a chair by the fire. Her round brown eyes were full of sleepy surprise. She said, "Who are you?"

"I'm Anne —"

"Anne what?"

Anne said, "I don't know."

"Do you mean you've lost your memory?"

"Yes."

"Oh — how odd —"

Anne said, "It's very uncomfortable."

"It must be. Would you like some tea?" Her tone was brightly matter-of-fact.

And then quite suddenly there came a knocking on the front door. Every scrap of colour left Anne's face. She had been pale before, now she looked as if only terror kept her alive. The girl nodded and said, "All right." She put out her hand to the electric light switch and turned it off.

The hope of darkness ... The words came into Anne's mind and stayed there. She was covered and protected. She remained standing, her hand on the back of an upright chair and her whole reliance on this little creature with the steady brown eyes. Five minutes ago she hadn't known of her existence, and now she was in the dark in a strange house, and all her reliance was upon this girl, younger than herself.

The girl went past her out of the room. The knocking on the front door came again.

A quiet came upon Anne. There were two things that might happen to her, and she saw them quite clearly. The girl could have gone upstairs to get away from her. She could have gone upstairs to her room, and she could lock herself in. And she could speak from her window and find out who was knocking at the door. And if she believed what he would say she would give Anne over to him.

Something in her mind refused to accept this as a possible happening. It didn't even frighten her very much. Perhaps that was because she was past being frightened either much or little. She waited, listening with all her ears — with more than her ears — with the whole of her, body and soul.

The tapping on the door came again.

This time it was followed by the sound of a window upstairs being thrown open. A sleepy voice called out, "Is that you, Aunt Hester?"

"Well, no —" It was a man's voice. It was his voice.

"Oh! What is it? What do you want?"

"I just wanted to enquire, have you seen or heard anything of my ward? She is missing."

"Your ward?"

"Yes. She's been ill. She's not fit to be out alone. If she's with you —"

"And what would make you think she was with me? If you've lost someone, go and look for her! Don't

120

come here, wakening me up and frightening me to death!"

The voice from the other side of the door became softer.

"I do apologize — I really do. If my niece is there —"

"Your niece is *not* here! How many more times do you want me to say that?"

"She isn't there?"

"No, she isn't!" The window above shut with a bang.

The man on the other side of the front door put his hand on the knocker. Anne heard it make a faint creak. Then his hand dropped again. He stood for a moment or two, and then she heard his footsteps going away down the path, down the four steps that led into the road. She heard him go, and she went on listening. Every sense seemed to be stretched. She could follow his footsteps in the road, she could hear him get into the car. He banged the door with a heavy decisive slam, and the car moved off, slowly at first, then quicker and quicker until it was gone.

Anne felt the stiffness go out of her. She hadn't realized how cold she was. It came over her now. She stood quite still where she was and waited, she didn't know for what. Now that it was over and he was gone, she groped her way to a chair and sat down, her head against the back of it and her eyes shut. She heard the girl come back into the room, dimly. She heard her voice, but she couldn't speak or answer. There was an interval — light in the room. It was warm — blessedly warm. Someone was shaking her by the shoulder. A voice was saying, "I've made some cocoa — you'd better have it."

She opened her eyes. She didn't know what a desperate appeal they held. She couldn't do any more than she had done. Her eyes said, "Help me — help me."

The little plump girl patted her shoulder.

"Drink this up and you'll feel better."

It was cocoa, warm and sweet. She drank it up. It seemed strange at first, but as she went on it was comfortable and warm. Her eyes were open and she was dazedly conscious of the room and the girl.

When she had finished the cup it was taken from her, and the girl said, "It was a good thing you locked the door when you came in. I had left it open — I'm awful about doing that. But the thing is, my aunt was coming back. She had been up to town for the day, and then when she rang up to say she'd met a friend and been persuaded to stay the night, I put off locking the door until I went to bed, and I sat down to read and went to sleep. And when I woke up I thought she'd come after all. It's an awful warning, isn't it?"

Anne blinked at her.

"I suppose it is. But if you hadn't left the door, I wouldn't have got in." She shuddered suddenly, violently.

The girl had a little painted tray in her hand. She scooped up the cup that had had the cocoa in it and laughed.

"I shan't tell Aunt Hester, or she'll preach like mad. She's all right, but she does hold forth." She put down

122

the tray and the cup and said briskly, "Now the thing is, what am I going to do with you. Have you got any ideas?"

Anne looked ahead and turned her eyes away. She couldn't do anything with tomorrow yet. Wait till it comes . . .

She was just going to speak when the girl said, "It's half-past one. I think we had better go to bed. I'll lend you a nightgown. It'll be rather short, but that doesn't matter. I always sleep with my feet tucked up. You can too. Then in the morning we can think about what we're going to do. My aunt won't be back till lunch-time, if then."

Anne took hold of the table edge to get up, but the effort spent itself, swept away by a flood of gratitude. She said in a low, stumbling voice, "That's good of you. You don't even know my name — I don't know it myself. I'm Anne, that's all I know."

"I'm Prissy — Prissy Knox. Come along up! You look as if you wanted a good sleep."

All at once Anne felt that was true. She got up. And that was the last thing she remembered at all clearly.

CHAPTER
TWENTY-THREE

When she looked back on it she could just remember going up the stairs, and that they seemed very steep. After that there was a candle-flame that worried her. It kept getting in her eyes. Her clothes seemed to be coming off. Prissy's little plump hands were undoing hooks and buttons and putting on a nightgown. And then — and then — the candle was being taken away and the room was dark about her. Prissy said something, she thought it was good-night, and the door shut. She sank into sleep like a stone sinking into water and there was nothing else at all.

At first her sleep was quite dreamless. She was too tired for thought. And then, as it drew near to morning and the dazed fatigue passed from her, the dreams came. She was running along a dark tunnel with the sound of an express train coming up behind her. She was sitting high up on a hillside with Jim. It was sunny, and they were at peace. It was like the time when they had been together on the last day she had seen him. She knew that there had been a last time, and she knew that he had taken her in his arms. He didn't touch her now. They sat side by side in the sunlight and did not look at one another. It was quite peaceful. And then the waves began to lap against their feet. Time seemed to have passed. There hadn't been any water, but time had passed and the sea was up to their feet. It filled all the place below them where she had seen the open fields and the trees. And suddenly a great wave broke over them. And Jim was gone. And she was alone. She came panting and struggling up from the dream into a crushing sense of loss. Jim was gone, and she was alone.

She opened her eyes and saw the strange room before she remembered anything. It frightened her. She started up in the grey, cold dawn and saw it. She had no memory of how she had come there, and for a moment everything was adrift. Then with a rush memory came back. She sat up in bed and saw herself coming downstairs in the other house, listening to the man as he talked to Lilian. She was back in the dark, her eyes wide, her heart thudding as she listened to them talking in the next room. She remembered it all. She could have repeated every word as she had heard, and every word said to her.

Get up and go from here as fast as you can. She was half out of bed, when there was a knock on the door and Prissy came in with her hair in a plait. It was absurd to feel caught, but she did.

Prissy was yawning.

"I hate getting up early," she said. "Don't you? It's only half-past six, but if you really want to catch a train —"

The train . . . She didn't know . . . She looked at Prissy for a moment of blank unseeing fear. And then it all cleared. She had to get away — to Jim — to Miss

Silver. She shut her eyes for a moment, and then opened them again.

"I'm sorry — I was dreaming. I don't know where I was, but not here."

"Are you here now?" There was a frank curiosity in Prissy's voice, and in her look too.

"Yes — I'm here —" Her voice shook a little on the words.

Prissy came over and sat on the bed.

"Well then, I think we'd better talk. What I thought was — you've got friends, haven't you?"

Jim — Miss Silver ... She said, "Yes, I've got friends."

Prissy hugged herself. She said with a good deal of relief, "Well, that's all right. I should think the best thing would be if I were to drive you to Felsham to catch a train. It's only seven miles, and it's a different line, so that if anyone wanted to catch you they wouldn't think of it — at least I hope they wouldn't."

"Would you — would you do that?"

"Yes, I would. Are you going to tell me anything?"

"I don't know. Would you believe me?"

Prissy burst out laughing.

"How can I tell? You can try. I mean, if you were to say you had fallen out of an aeroplane, or something like that, I might help you, but I shouldn't believe you, because that would be stupid. It would be much easier to believe that you were making it up, or — or something like that."

Anne looked at her. Bright brown eyes in a rosy face, a red dressing-gown, bare feet tucked up beneath her.

126

She said, "I won't make anything up, I promise you that. I can't tell you everything, because I've lost my memory and I don't know it myself. If I tell you what I do remember you'll maybe not believe me, so I think I won't. Because they'll tell lies — the man who came here last night —"

"Yes, who is he?"

"I don't know — I really don't."

Prissy had her arms round her knees. She giggled a little and said, "He said you were his niece."

"I know — I heard him. It isn't true."

"How do you know if you can't remember?"

"I'd never seen him before — I'm sure I hadn't. He was utterly strange and — and horrible."

Prissy was nodding.

"Yes, I thought so too. I was glad you'd locked the door. I thought he was a horror." She got off the bed and yawned. "Isn't getting up beastly? But we'd better get going before there are too many people about."

Anne got out of bed and dressed quickly. She had ten pounds not broken into, that was her real comfort. Ten pounds. She looked for her bag, and couldn't see it.

It wasn't there.

She stared about the room, unbelieving. She was still staring when Prissy came back. Anne lifted eyes full of tragedy and said, "My money is gone —"

"Oh — when did you have it last?"

"I don't know. It was in my bag — I can't see it. It was in notes — ten one-pound notes."

"When can you remember seeing it last?"

Anne tried to think.

"Yesterday morning." She sat down on the bed, her face white, her hands shaking. "What am I going to do?"

"Perhaps you left it downstairs."

They looked downstairs, but there was nothing there.

Prissy marched out of the room. Before Anne could get hold of herself she was back again. She had a little bunch of notes in her hand.

"Here you are," she said.

The colour came back into Anne's face with a rush. She said, "Oh, Prissy, I can't!"

Prissy screwed up her face.

"Nonsense! Money's only any good when it's doing something. This isn't any good at all, not whilst I've got it, because it's not doing anything but sitting in a box under my nightgowns. If that horrid man of yours had got in last night he'd have taken it." She gave a determined little nod of the head. "Quite easily. Come along, we'll have some breakfast. And then we'll be off to the train."

They had cold bacon and bread and marmalade and cocoa for breakfast. And then Prissy went down to the garage and got out the car.

"And suppose the horror is prowling. I think you had better be very quick. In fact I think it would be a good thing if you sort of crouched down in the back seat with a rug over you, so that no one would know I wasn't alone. And the sooner we get off the better."

Anne was stiff with fear. The sense of not knowing who she was, of being naked and open to attack, was strong upon her. All the way to Felsham she clutched the rug round her and thought with horror of letting go of it and stepping out on to the platform.

When they reached the first houses Prissy said, "You'd better come out now. It won't do to look as if you didn't want to be seen."

That was true. She pushed away the rug, sat up, and tidied her hair. She was more frightened than she had been at all, but she mustn't show it.

The car ran down to the station, drew up, and she got out. When she turned round Prissy was getting out too. She said, "Go into the waiting-room. It's just here. I'll take your ticket."

It was a game for Prissy, an exciting game. But for her — And then suddenly there was a rush of courage and hope. She walked into the waiting-room and sat down with her back to the light.

Prissy came to her there with the ticket.

"Here you are. There's a quarter of an hour before the train comes in. It sounds horrid, but I think I had better not wait."

Anne threw a startled look.

"Why?"

"Mrs Brown," said Prissy. "It's her day. If she comes and finds me out she'll talk about it all over the place. As it is, if I go at once I shall just get back before she comes and there won't be any talk. You'll be all right." She nodded her head and took both of Anne's cold hands in hers, which were like little warm pies.

"Let me know how it all comes out," she said, and was gone.

CHAPTER
TWENTY-FOUR

Prissy drove back in a very good humour. She was pleased with herself. She thought of telling Aunt Hester that they had had a visitor, but decided that she wouldn't. Aunt Hester was all right, but she was inclined to fuss, and she hadn't seen Anne. It would be better if she didn't say anything about her. Aunt Hester wasn't very practical, yet she had had at least thirty years more of reading the papers than Prissy had. She knew a terrible lot about shady characters and tricks, and all sorts of things which oughtn't to be but tried to pretend that they were. If you read too many of those things they get in the way of what you really know about people — of what a cat or a dog knows, or a child.

Prissy considered that she was very good at judging people and knowing what they were really like. That man last night, she had really hated him from the first moment that he knocked on the door. Anne was all right — Prissy had been quite sure about that from the first moment. She was sorry not to have seen her onto the train, but the sensible thing was to come away at once and not let anyone see them together, and then to get home before Mrs Brown came. She went along at a pleasant speed and sang to herself.

She had locked the garage door and let herself into the house, when it came to her suddenly that she had been very wise. She was quite often pleased with herself, but this time she was very pleased indeed, because not a quarter of an hour after she had let herself into the house there was someone tapping on the front door again. It was too early for Mrs Brown. A quarter past eight was her time, and it was only eight o'clock.

She went down, and she put the chain on the door before she opened it. It was the first time she had ever used the chain, and she was very glad of it. The door opened as far as the chain would let it, and she saw the man who was standing outside.

Horrid. Casual. Impertinent. A bad lot.

She said, "What is it?" He said, "Well, I'm looking for a lost lady. I came here last night, but you weren't very hospitable. Now that it's quite respectably daylight, don't you think you might open the door? I'm enquiring for Miss Fancourt, just up the road from you."

She wasn't taken in for a minute. He was a bad lot. She wished she had something to stand on, because he was right up over her head. She stood up as tall as she could and said, "I don't know what you're talking about. My aunt's in town, and Mrs Brown won't be here for a quarter of an hour. Please go away."

"Well, then I shall just have to wait and see Mrs Brown, that's all. You're making a bit of an ass of yourself, you know. If you've got the girl here, you can't keep her. She's in Miss Fancourt's charge, and she isn't right in the head, that's all. You're taking a very great responsibility in keeping her away from the people who are looking after her."

Just for one awful moment there was a most horrible waggle in Prissy's mind. Suppose what he said was true. It wasn't the black dark of night any longer. It was broad daylight — well, not so very broad, because there was a black cloud over them, and it looked as if it might be going to rain at any moment. Everything in her shook.

And then quite suddenly everything was steady again. She believed Anne, and she didn't believe a single word this creature was saying. She looked over her shoulder at the hall clock and saw that it was seven minutes past eight. She said, "That's all very well, but I'm not supposed to open the door to anyone when I'm alone like this. You'll have to wait till Mrs Brown comes."

He didn't want to wait. She heard him say "Damn!" quite distinctly through the door. She said, "She'll be here in about five minutes, I should think. Do you mind if I shut the door?" and she shut it right in his face.

It was a very rude thing to do. Part of her was shocked, and part of her was very pleased. There was something extraordinarily gratifying about being rude to someone who couldn't get at you. She tingled with excitement and backed away from the door.

It was a very long five minutes, and right in the middle of it Prissy had the most dreadful idea. Suppose that this day, out of all the days in the month and all the months in the year, Mrs Brown shouldn't come! She was firm with herself. Why shouldn't she come? She would come — she'd got to come — she always came.

The voice from the other side of the door broke in, "Look here, this is nonsense!" The man outside was very angry.

Mrs Brown would be here in a minute. She would be a great help. Prissy went back until her heels struck against the first step of the stairs. The man was banging on the door and shaking the handle. She went up two or three steps and waited for Mrs Brown. When it was over it would be an adventure. In all her eighteen years she had never had an adventure like this before.

From the other side of the front door she could hear the man stop his knocking. She heard the gate. She heard Mrs Brown say, "Why, what's up?" and she ran down the three steps and along the passage to the back door.

"Mrs Brown! Mrs Brown!"

Mrs Brown made short work of him.

"Scaring the life out of a young girl! Really, you should be ashamed of yourself! No, you'll not come in! If you've anything to say, you can say it to Miss Hester Knox when she comes home! There's no one in the house corresponding to what you say! There's no one here but myself and Miss Prissy that you've scared into a come-over!"

Prissy listened to her in full blast. She wasn't in a come-over, but her legs felt a bit waggledy and she was quite pleased to sit down on the stairs and listen to Mrs Brown putting it across the horrid man. She didn't think she was going to tell Mrs Brown about Anne. She thought she had better not. She didn't think she was going to tell Aunt Hester. Really, the fewer people who knew the better. Aunt Hester would certainly tell her great friend Miss Ribblesdale, and goodness knew how many people Miss Ribblesdale might confide in. Come to think of it Aunt Hester wasn't so bad, but Miss Ribblesdale had hundreds of friends absent and present. Absent friends didn't matter so much. The present ones did. Why, before you could turn round everyone in Haleycott would know. Prissy had a horrifyingly clear picture of Mrs Bodingley, and Miss Escott, and Mrs Town, and the two Miss Bamfields all talking like mad. She shook her head in a very determined way and made up her mind that they weren't going to talk about her — or Anne. She got up from the stairs and said, "Oh, Mrs Brown, what a horrid man! He said he was looking for someone — his niece he said she was. And why he should have come here, I can't think, with Aunt Hester away and all."

Mrs Brown looked shocked.

"Miss Knox is away?"

"Well, just for the night. She'll be back for lunch — at least I suppose she will."

Mrs Brown took off her hat and coat and hung them on the pegs in the scullery.

"You did quite right keeping him in his place like you did, my dear. A horrid low fellow, that's what he was. I thought as I'd do the dining-room and your aunt's bedroom this morning — give them a good clear-out. And we'll have a cup of tea before we start. I'm sure you look quite pale, Miss Prissy."

Prissy did feel a little pale.

CHAPTER
TWENTY-FIVE

Anne sat in the train. The escape feeling was strong on her. She had done it. She had got away. Nothing could stop her. All these well-known feelings surged in her and had their way — for about half an hour.

It was then that she began to think. What was she going to do and where was she going to go? She thought about Jim. Suppose she went to him. Well, suppose she did, and he didn't believe her. This was a most dreadful thought, and she made herself think about it quietly and steadily. What, after all, did he know about her? Only that she had turned up with his wife's bag and with an incredible tale of seeing her lying dead in the cellar of a strange house. If she could have given any account of herself, if she could have said where she had come from and what she was doing — if she even knew her own real name — But she didn't know anything at all except that her Christian name was Anne. Her memory was gone, and she didn't know if it would ever come back. It might, or it might not — she couldn't tell. How could she go to Jim? The answer was perfectly plain. If he believed Lilian — and why shouldn't he believe her — she was lost. Something in her which was proud and independent roused up and took possession of her. Not yet. She must find somewhere where she could be quiet for a little. Jim had left her with his aunts, and she had come away. She wouldn't go back, no matter what he said or did. And if she wouldn't go back she must take a little time to consider what she would do.

She put Jim away from her and thought about Miss Silver. Could she go to Miss Silver? She had to think that out very carefully, because if she couldn't — if she couldn't — A spasm of terror swept over her. Her hands came together in her lap and clenched there. Could she go to Miss Silver? And as she put the question she knew very well what the answer must be — she couldn't. The answer came with a terrible distinctness, and not all the shrinking of her flesh and spirit could interfere with its clarity. Miss Silver was working with Jim. She couldn't, she mustn't, risk it. She dared not risk it. If she had had her memory clear — if . . . What was the good of that? The face of the man who had come to her in the garden came up in her memory. It was fearfully distinct. He might say anything, and she couldn't contradict him of her own knowledge. He could say anything he liked, and she would be helpless. Her mind showed her one thing after another that he might say, and she would know that they couldn't be true, but she could not prove them untrue — she couldn't prove anything at all. Then if she couldn't disprove his lies, what was she to do? Disappear — vanish into the crowds of London. That was the only safe way until her memory came back.

And suppose it never did come back? A tremor ran over her. No use to think about the future.

Quite suddenly a picture came up in her mind. It was the picture of a little girl eight or nine years old writing in a copy-book. What she wrote was, "Manners makyth man". She had got down about half-way on the page — "Manners makyth man", over and over again. The picture was small and clear. Suddenly the child stopped writing, stretched out her right hand, and gave a deep sigh. The picture vanished. But in that moment Anne had recognised herself. It was Aunt Letty who set those copies, and as the words went through her mind she saw Aunt Letty quite plainly, a mountainous creature, quite old, with white hair and a hard hand that was quick to slap.

The whole hadn't lasted a minute. It left her grasping but encouraged. She had remembered. For the first time the curtain had lifted. It would certainly have been of more use if it had lifted on some nearer scene. But curiously enough that picture of herself as a child of eight and a half or nine was most oddly reassuring. To look back and see herself as a child brought the present, as it were, into focus.

Her hands relaxed, and her mind quietened. She had ten pounds, and she had her freedom. Now that she had started remembering she would go on. There was nothing to be dismayed about. Everything would come right.

It was curious the effect it had on her. She felt hopeful and encouraged. For the rest of the way her mind was full of plans. She must get work. The money

Prissy had given her wouldn't last her for very long. She must get a room, and she must buy a nightgown and a brush and comb. She would have to pay for her room in advance. Oh, and she must have a case of some sort. Quite a cheap one would do — but no one would take you in without any luggage.

She went on planning.

CHAPTER
TWENTY-SIX

Jim rang up Chantreys about an hour later.

"I'd like to speak to Anne."

There was a curious effect. He couldn't make out what it was. The nearest he got to it was dismay. It was Lilian who had answered. First she didn't say anything at all, then she said, "Anne —"

"Yes."

"Well —"

"I want to speak to her."

Lilian didn't know what to do. She temporized.

"I don't know that you can."

"Why?"

"She — she isn't here."

"You mean she's out?"

"Well —"

"Lilian, do you mind telling me what you mean?"

There was a pause. She was greatly tempted to hang up. She could pretend they had been cut off. Her mind, twisting this way and that, boggled at a decision.

"Jim — something has happened."

It was a relief to tell him. He would have to be told. Much better to tell the truth — really —

"What has happened?"

140

"She — she's gone."

"Lilian, what do you mean?"

"She — she's gone. I couldn't stop her. I didn't know she was going."

"Do you mean that Anne has gone?"

Lilian's voice became more and more agitated.

"Yes — yes. And it's no use your asking me why, for I don't know any more about it than you do. When we got up this morning she wasn't here, that's all — she just wasn't here. And it's no good asking why she went off like that, because I don't know. No one here knows. I said good-night to her, and she went up to bed, and that's the last I saw of her — the very last."

Lilian was quite pleased with herself by now. She had got over the worst of it. Jim couldn't really say anything. He had deceived her shamefully. She didn't know whether to say anything about that to him or not. Perhaps better not. What was it that man had said last night — "Least said, soonest mended." Yes, that was what she had got to remember. When you hadn't said anything you could always put in a word here and there just as it might be convenient. She became aware of Jim's voice, very hard and cold — "I'm coming down at once." And then the click of the receiver being replaced.

By the time that Jim arrived Lilian was quite persuaded that she could carry everything off just as she wanted to. She was one of those people who can work out a fine plan if there is no one else to call the tune, but with Jim facing her it wasn't so easy. To begin with, she had never seen him like this before. She had not seen very much of him. He had been brought up by his mother's family, and on his visits he had been at first the boy and then the rather silent young man. Then he had vanished for three years — they really didn't know what he had been doing. It was nonsense to think of his embarrassing them, and she certainly wasn't going to stand it.

And then when he came down everything seemed to have changed. He was a man now, he wasn't a boy any longer. When he looked at her like this her heart contracted. She couldn't help it.

She got up, walked to the window, and back again.

"I don't know what you think. I'm sure we were all as kind to her as we could be."

"Were you? Then why did she go?"

"*Really* — how do I know? You can say what you like, but there was something very extraordinary about her. I don't know, I'm sure —"

He stood in front of the fireplace and looked at her.

"What don't you know?"

"*Really*, Jim, anyone would think —"

"What would they think?"

Lilian burst into tears.

"Anyone would think you — you suspected us! It's very hard — it's very *hard*!"

"Lilian — do you know why she went?"

"No, I don't."

"Then I must see whether anyone else does."

And he was gone. It was a relief, but what did he mean to do? She couldn't think. She blew her nose and went over what she had said. There was nothing the matter. He couldn't expect her to know anything. He couldn't think that she did know anything. It would be all right. It *must* be all right. And if he had gone . . . Had he gone?

He had not gone.

When he left Lilian's room he made his way to the back premises. It was in his mind that he would see Thomasina. Lilian was always concerned with making a smooth tale. He didn't want smooth tales, he wanted the truth. He thought that he would get it from Thomasina.

He came across her in the pantry and shut the door.

"Thomasina, I want to ask you about Mrs Fancourt."

She turned round to him with a teapot in her hand and a fine polishing cloth.

"Yes, Mr Jim?"

"I hear she's gone."

"So it would seem." The words came without fuss, slowly — he thought with something in the voice. No, he couldn't get nearer to it than that.

He said, "Do you know why she went?"

Thomasina rubbed at the side of the teapot.

"I might form a guess, sir."

"What would be your guess?"

"I don't know that I should say."

"Yes, you must say."

She went on rubbing the teapot. Presently she said, "It's not my place to talk of what goes on in the house."

He leaned forward and took her wrists in a light, steady clasp.

"I'm not talking about what is your place and what isn't. I'm talking about my desperate need to know what has happened to Anne."

She lifted her eyes to his and said steadily, "It's like that, is it?"

"Yes, it's like that."

She turned round and put the teapot down without haste, without fuss. Then when she was facing him again she looked at him and said, "She's good."

"Yes, she's good."

He had the feeling that they were talking on a different plane now. It was the plane on which you spoke the simple truth and it was received as such. Everything was plain and easy between them. He said, "Why did she go?"

"I don't know. She went in a hurry."

"How do you know that?"

She took her time to answer. Her eyes were on his face. When she spoke her voice wasn't quite so calm.

"I woke up out of my first sleep — I don't generally wake. It went through my head that there was something to be done and that I hadn't known what it was. And then sleep came over me again, and I didn't wake till it was light."

He heard what she said. It didn't mean anything — or it meant too much. Which was it? He said, "When did you find out that she was gone?"

"When I went in with her tea. The blind was pulled back like she always had it, and I could see at once that she wasn't there. Nor her clothes. Her hat and coat were gone as well as the rest. But she'd left her bag."

"Was her purse in it?"

Thomasina shook her head.

"She didn't have a purse. The notes was in the middle of the bag, and a little loose change in the pocket at the side. I looked to see." Her voice was quite calm and decided.

He called out sharply, "But if she hadn't any money with her, how could she go?"

"I don't know." There was something in her voice — something.

He said, "Thomasina, if there is anything at all, you must tell me — you *must*."

She looked at him full.

"I don't know, and that's the truth — I don't know anything. But the back door was open this morning. It wasn't Mattie or me who left it open."

"Why would she go out the back way?"

"Seems to me it would be because she didn't want to be heard."

"Yes. But what made her — what made her?"

Thomasina had her thoughts, but she kept them close. Getting no answer, Jim sought one of himself.

"Something must have happened. That time you woke up — when would it be?"

"I don't know. I don't generally wake before the middle of the night."

"That would be between twelve and one?"

She nodded. "But it's nothing to go by."

"What could have happened to make her go off like that? She went in a hurry — because she forgot her bag. How could she have forgotten it?"

145

Thomasina's eyes met his.

"I don't know."

He turned from her and stood for a moment with his face averted. Then he swung round on her again.

"There must have been something to make her go off like that."

Thomasina said slowly, "Perhaps she remembered something."

CHAPTER
TWENTY-SEVEN

Jim went straight back to Miss Silver.

"No one knows anything about her. She has simply vanished," he said.

Miss Silver picked up her knitting and sat in silence for a minute or two. Then she looked up at him standing on her hearthrug and said, "It would be better if you sat down, Mr Fancourt."

"I don't feel as if I could."

"Nevertheless it will be better . . . Thank you. What do you think has happened?"

"I don't know. I've thought the whole way up on the train. It seems to me there are only two ways of it. Either she went off herself, or she was taken."

"That is reasonable."

"If she went off herself, why did she leave her purse?"

"She could have been in a very great hurry."

"What hurry?"

"That we do not know. But you say that yesterday when you went down something had happened."

"Yes, that man had come down and found her in the garden. He had threatened her. But she didn't know him, she didn't know him at all. She had never seen him before. What he said was a complete mystery to her."

"What did he say?"

"He said they'd got to have a talk. He said they wouldn't want to have it in public. He frightened her. She turned quite faint when he said it. He laughed at her and said that she knew what he might say, and she said she didn't know — she didn't know anything. She said, 'I think that's what frightened me. If I could have remembered, I wouldn't have been so frightened. It's not knowing, not being able to see. It's like waking up in the night and not knowing where you are.'" He repeated the words, and they brought her close to him. He wasn't in here with Miss Silver. He was out on the windy side of the hill. His arm was round her. He felt her tremble against him.

Miss Silver knitted. She knew very well where he was. She let him be there. Presently he began to speak again.

"After a little she went on — telling me what he said. I don't know whether he mistook her for somebody else, but what he said was, 'Remember, we know who you are.' Then he said he'd got some orders for her. She wasn't to tell anyone she'd seen him, or what he had said. And when she got her orders she was to do just what she was told, and at once. Then he said, 'You'd better,' and turned round and went away."

Miss Silver looked up.

"She did not know him at all?"

"Not at all."

"I see —" She paused for thought.

148

Jim's voice came in.

"I can't understand it — any of it. You know how it is. You're near someone — very near. You know they're speaking the truth. And when I say you know, I mean you really do know. There's no guess work about it — there's only one mind between you. Well, it was like that." He sat back in his chair.

Miss Silver inclined her head gently. She said, "I see."

He went on.

"And then all of a sudden there's a complete break — you can't get in touch with them any more. It's plain hell. What happened — that's what I keep on trying to get at. What could possibly have happened?"

Miss Silver knitted in silence for a minute or two. Then she said, "It seems to me that there are two alternatives. One is that Anne has recovered her memory. We do not know what that memory may have shown her."

"Do you think that?"

"I do not know. It is evident that something of an extremely disturbing nature occurred. Will you tell me just what happened between you?"

He told her.

She said, "The other alternative is that something happened after you left — something that made her decide to get away. Can you think of anything that she may possibly have learned?"

He said, "She went in a great hurry."

He reminded her about the abandoned bag.

"Then she had no money with her?"

"None. As far as we know."

There was another silence. Then Miss Silver said, "What sort of woman is your aunt?"

"Lilian?"

"If that is her name."

"There are two of them. Lilian and Harriet. Harriet is the younger. She is entirely taken up with local good works."

"The letter which was in Anne's handbag was signed Lilian. What kind of woman is she?"

Jim stared.

"I've never seen very much of either of them. State visits at intervals — you know the kind of thing. She's not a brain. She is just a woman living in the country."

In Miss Silver's mind was a clear recollection of something which her friend at Haleycott had said about Lilian Fancourt — "One of those women who haven't got very much, but what they've got they stick to."

"And, if I may ask you — what is the position with regard to the house at Haleycott?"

Jim said slowly, "My grandfather left it to me, but — I wouldn't have turned them out. They'd lived there always. They were the second family. It wouldn't have been right to turn them out."

"Did they know that?"

"I suppose they knew what my grandfather's will was. Look here, Miss Silver, you can't think —"

She fixed her eyes upon his face.

"I think that no avenue must be unexplored."

He got up from his chair. It was as if he pushed the whole thing away.

150

"Look here, we can't go into that. If Lilian wanted to do anything, what could she do? Besides, she isn't like that. She's a fussy, silly woman. I don't mind telling you a little of her goes a long way with me. But when all's said and done, what could she do?"

"Mr Fancourt, did this man who came see her?"

"See Lilian? Yes, he did. But I don't know that he asked for her. Thomasina wasn't sure whether he said Mrs Fancourt or Miss Fancourt."

"And was he with her long?"

"Thomasina didn't know. She went back to her pantry. She left him with Lilian."

They went on talking, and got nowhere.

CHAPTER
TWENTY-EIGHT

The train got into the terminus. Anne left it. She did not know where she was going. She did not know what she was going to do. She went and sat down in the waiting-room and tried to think. For a long time nothing came to her. Then she began to think.

She got up and walked out of the station. She had to buy a suitcase, and she had to find a room. She got the suitcase almost at once, and then bought herself a cheap nightgown, brush and comb, a cake of soap, and a towel. It was terrifying how much things cost, but no one would take her in without luggage. A curious feeling pushed up through her consciousness. These were not the sort of things she had ever bought before. She could do a sum in her head. She could know that she mustn't spend more than the least possible, but all the time she knew in her own mind that these were not the sort of things she had ever bought before. It was all new to her, this considering of prices, this taking the cheapest thing that was offered.

In the first shop she went into she began to give her name. She got as far as Miss Anne, and stopped dead and bit her lip.

"No, I'll pay for it," she said.

The girl who was serving her with the nightdress looked up at her with a quick fleeting glance.

When she had got as much as she dared, she turned her attention to the question of a room. There was a policeman at the next crossing. She made her way to him, waited till he was disengaged from the traffic, and then put her request.

"Can you tell me where I can get a room?"

The policeman was comfortable-looking. Ten years before, he had come up to London. The country burr still lingered in his voice. He said, "What kind of a room, miss?"

And Anne said, "A very cheap one."

He directed her to a Young Woman's Christian, and it sounded frightfully respectable and safe. She went on her way feeling very clever and encouraged. Nothing happened to you if you were sensible.

Nothing could possibly happen to you at a Young Woman's Christian. It sounded too utterly respectable and safe. She would deposit her luggage — how safe and respectable to have luggage — and she would ask them about jobs. They would know. The mere fact that there was going to be someone whom she could ask was like light in a dark place — the dark place of her ignorance, of her not knowing.

But the Young Woman's Christian was full. They gave her one or two addresses and said they might be able to take her in next week. She embarked on a long and weary hunt for a room. At last, too tired to be particular, she took what was offered by a woman whom she would have turned down flat at the beginning of her search, a little carneying person with untidy hair and a smooth ingratiating way of speech. She didn't know how long she would want the room for, and she would leave her things there and go out and get something to eat. She was tired to the very bones of her, and she was so discouraged that there seemed to be no place left for her either to fall or to rise. The world was an empty place. There was no one who cared whether she was alive or dead. "Let us eat and drink; for tomorrow we die."

She ate and drank in a dirty little shop, and then she went back to her room and undressed and went to bed. The day had begun early and there had not been much of the night. She put on her clean nightgown and lay down in the doubtful bed wondering if she would sleep, and that was the last thing she knew until the morning. She slept and slept, and when she woke she was conscious of nothing. The hours of sleep had passed over her and were gone.

Her depression was gone too. She must find a job. And she must write to Jim and Miss Silver. It wasn't fair to leave them without a word. She had got away, and now that she was quite on her own she could see them again. It was a very heartening thought. She put on her coat and hat, considered whether she could ask Jim to get hold of her bag and her money from Chantreys, and set out first on a quest for a roll and butter and a cup of tea, and then to look for a job.

CHAPTER
TWENTY-NINE

Miss Silver got the letter with her breakfast next day. It was the second in a pile of letters. She opened it first. She read:

Dear Miss Silver,

I am writing to tell you that I had to come away. I couldn't help it. When I see you I will tell you, but I don't know when that will be. I've got to get work before I do anything else. I thought I must write to you because of Jim. I meant to write to him, but I couldn't. He will be so very angry with me for coming away, and I don't know whether I could tell him why. I must think it well over first. But if you see him, or if he comes to you, will you *please* tell him not to worry. He was so very good to me — as you were. It would be a bad return if I did anything that would make things difficult for him. I will send you an address when I have got one. This is only temporary. Dear Miss Silver, I feel so grateful to you. I can't explain, but please, *please* do believe that I don't mean to be ungrateful, and that I am all right.

The letter was signed "Anne".

Miss Silver read it through twice, then she left the breakfast-table, went into her sitting-room, and rang up Jim Fancourt.

"Mr Fancourt —"

"Yes — who is it?"

"It is Miss Silver. I have a letter from Anne."

She read it aloud to him, and he received it in silence. After a moment she said, "Mr Fancourt, are you there?"

She got an angry laugh.

"Oh, yes, I'm here — and a lot of use that seems to be! She says she writes from London?"

"Yes."

"Why does she not write to me?"

Miss Silver looked at the letter again. She said, "I think there has been trouble with your aunt."

"What makes you think that?"

"It is an impression."

"Something must have caused it."

"Yes. She says she had to come away, she could not help it. Then what she says of you — 'He will be so very angry with me for coming away, and I don't know whether I could tell him why. I must think it well over first.'" She read on to the end of the letter, and then returned to the sentence which said, "It would be a bad return if I did anything that would make things more difficult for him." "That appears to me to be her motive — not to make things difficult for you."

"Damned little fool!"

Miss Silver turned a deaf ear. She could not approve of "language", but she could ignore it. She said, "I will send you a copy of this letter. It will, I think, be a satisfaction to you to have it, and I will let you know at once when I hear from her again."

When Jim received the letter he read it through more than enough times to know it by heart. She said, "I meant to write to him but I couldn't." Why on earth couldn't she? She could tell him anything — anything. Why could she tell Miss Silver what she couldn't tell him? He went on reading. "He will be so very angry with me for coming away, and I don't think I can tell him why. I must think it well over first." And what did she mean by that? What had she got to think over? "Will you please tell him not to worry." Not to worry — "He was so very good to me. It would be a bad return if I did anything that would make things difficult for him." What was at the back of all this? And she had left her bag with the money in it. That was the real puzzle. You can't get anywhere without money, but she had got to London. How? How had she gone? He could imagine ways, but they infuriated him. And where was she now? In London? She might be, or she might not.

He rang Miss Silver up.

"Jim Fancourt speaking. You haven't heard any more?"

"No, Mr Fancourt. I will let you know as soon as I do."

"You think you will hear?"

"I am sure I shall."

157

Her quiet, firm voice was reassuring. He said, "I don't know where to look for her — I don't know what to do."

Miss Silver said, "There is nothing you can do except wait."

"That's the damnable thing."

"I will ring you up as soon as I hear anything."

CHAPTER
THIRTY

On the third day of her search for work Anne was obliged to contend with discouragement. People wanted to know what you had been doing, and she didn't know herself. She began to wonder whether she couldn't make up something, but really when you came to look into it there was altogether too much to make up. If it had only been her name — if she could only produce one person who could speak for her — She thought of Miss Silver, at first to feel that she couldn't ask her for a reference, but with each successive day to come nearer and nearer to trying her. "But she doesn't really know anything about me." And then, hard on that, "Nobody does —" The thought took her into a sort of giddy spin. For a moment she was all alone with no one to help her. No one who knew who she was or where she was. It was like being giddy, only much, much worse. She was out in the street when it happened to her, and she had to stand still and let the crowd go by. She groped her way to a railing and stood there till her head cleared. She must never let herself think like that again. She would remember — some day. And meanwhile she must go on —

And then someone was speaking to her. A voice said, "Are you feeling ill?" and she lifted her head and saw a girl of about her own age looking at her with concern.

"No, I'm all right — now."

The girl said in a deep, strong voice, "You don't look all right to me. Come in and have a cup of tea. There's a shop just here."

Anne felt a curious relief. Here was someone else making a decision for her. The girl slipped a hand in a rather shabby dark brown glove inside her arm, and she turned and went with her no more than a dozen steps along the pavement, where they turned, and another dozen steps. There was an interval when she really didn't know what was happening, and then her head cleared and she lifted it. She was sitting on a bench with a little marble-topped table in front of her. Her head was almost down upon her hands. The girl was speaking to her.

"Are you better? I should keep my head down a little longer. Can you take cocoa — because that's what I've ordered. You look as if it would do you good. Don't bother to answer if it's all right."

Anne felt relaxed and relieved. A curious indifference seemed to have come over her. She didn't know it, but she was almost at the end of her strength. This girl could take over for a time. There was nothing she herself could do.

When the cocoa came she drank it and came slowly back. The girl was looking at her with frank curiosity.

"What on earth have you been doing to yourself?"

Anne said, "I don't know."

"Do you mean that?"

"Yes, I do. I don't know who I am."

The girl pursed her lips and whistled.

"I say, that's bad! You don't really mean that, do you?"

"Yes, I do."

"But how?"

Anne found herself telling her. Not all of it. Not about the girl at the foot of the steps. She began where she got on to the bus and met Miss Silver. When she got to Chantreys, she found herself in difficulties. She had to leave Jim out. Curiously enough, that hurt. It hurt so much that she didn't know how to do it. She stopped, and looked at the girl. She didn't know what a hurt, shocked look it was, but the girl said quickly, "Just leave out anything you don't want to say."

Anne's look melted in gratitude.

"It's difficult —" she said under her breath.

The girl said quickly, "Don't tell me anything you don't want to."

"I — I had to come away again — in the middle of the night. It — it wasn't my fault."

"What did you do?"

"A girl took me in till the early morning. Then I came up to town."

The round eyes gave her a searching look.

"Had you anywhere to go?"

Anne shook her head.

The girl said, "Now you must eat something. Those are quite plain buns." And, when Anne had helped herself, "What did you do?"

"I found a room. It took nearly all day."

The girl frowned.

"You don't sound enthusiastic."

Anne gave her the sort of smile which breaks into tears before you know where you are. She felt it going that way and bit her lip quickly.

"It isn't the sort of room that anyone could feel enthusiastic about. It was — dirty. So was the landlady."

The girl frowned more deeply.

"Don't you know anyone?"

Anne said, "Miss Silver."

The girl clapped her hands together.

"Is that the same Miss Silver I know about? She's better than dozens of references!"

Anne said, "15 Montague Mansions," and the girl clapped her hands again and burst out laughing.

"That's the one — the one and only! I've only met her once, but she did wonderful things for a cousin of mine, Evelyn Baring, so you see we're introduced, all quite properly. My name is Janet Wells. And yours is Anne — Anne what?"

The colour rose in Anne's face.

"I've been calling myself Anne Fancourt. I think the Anne part of it is right. The other isn't, but one must have a surname."

Janet frowned.

"Look here, you can't stay in that horrid dirty room you're in. I'll come with you and get your things, and if you'd like to — well, there's a room in the house we're in. One of the girls went away last week, and the room wasn't let when I came out this morning. So if you'd like —"

Anne put out a hand and half drew it back again. She didn't know how her eyes lighted up.

"You don't know anything about me," she said in a shaking voice. "Miss Silver doesn't either — not really — only since she met me."

Janet Wells took the hand, held it firmly for a moment, patted it, and let it go again.

"You'd do as much for me, I expect," she said in a plain matter-of-fact sort of voice.

CHAPTER
THIRTY-ONE

It is much easier to be firm for somebody else than for oneself. Mrs Pink was all set to be disagreeable, and Anne hadn't come out of feeling dazed. It was easier to give way, to pay what she asked, and have done with it. But Janet Wells wasn't having any. She said just what she thought and she stuck to it, and in the end they got away.

When they were in a taxi with Anne's suitcase, Janet turned to her.

"That's a nasty woman. You ought never to have gone there."

"I know. I'd been up half the night, and everywhere I went they seemed to be full. I — I must seem dreadfully stupid. I — I'm not always like this — I'm not really."

"Of course you're not. Don't worry about it. Don't worry about anything."

A sense of being looked after came comfortingly in upon Anne. She leaned back in the taxi and closed her eyes. She wasn't sure whether she dropped off or not, she thought perhaps she had. But all of a sudden she came to with a start. The taxi had pulled up, and Janet's hand was on her knee.

"Anne — we're here."

She was still a little dazed as she paid the fare and followed Janet up the front steps of a big house in a square. There were names on brass plates. The hall had linoleum down, and there was linoleum on the stairs. Janet put a hand on the handle of the suitcase and said, "Come along up. We're on the second floor. The room you can have is one floor higher up, but you can share our sitting-room if you like. Here, what's the matter? Are you faint again?"

Anne was leaning against the banisters. She wasn't holding the bag any more. It had slipped from her hand. Janet let go of the handle and put a firm, strong arm round her.

"Sit down. Put your head down. I'll get you up when you're better. There's no hurry."

"I'm so sorry." The words were only just audible. She heard the sound of running steps and fainted away.

When she came to she was on a sofa in what had been the drawing-room of the house, or the front half of it. There were voices in the room. One of them was saying, "Well, I think you're mad." To which Janet answered, "All right, so I'm mad. And that's the way I am."

Anne turned on to her side and saw the two girls over by the window. As she moved, Janet detached herself and came towards her.

"Are you better? Don't try and talk until you've had something to eat. You've been starving yourself. You're going to have soup and custard pudding, and there's an awfully good cheese — Oh, this is my cousin Lizabet."

165

Anne began, "I'm so dreadfully sorry. You must think —" Her voice failed her.

Lizabet had remained turned away. Now she swung round.

"I want to say —" she began, and Janet interrupted her. "You don't want to say anything at all!"

Anne was conscious of a sharp disagreement. She struggled up on her elbow and said, "Oh!" She looked at Lizabet and Lizabet looked at her. Anne didn't know herself what she looked like. If she had thought about it she would have said untidy — dishevelled. That wasn't what came into Janet's mind, but defenceless — innocent. Anne went on looking at Lizabet as one does in those defenceless moments. "Why — why?" And then, "How lovely she is."

Lizabet said, "Why do you look at me like that?"

A little faint colour came into Anne's face. She said, "I'm sorry. You're so pretty."

Lizabet turned colour. Janet said, "Yes, isn't she? Come along, Lizabet, and help me with her lunch."

Lizabet went.

Anne pulled herself up on the sofa and looked about her. She felt weak and free. She felt that Janet was a tower of strength. And Lizabet — what was she — an enemy? The words came into her mind and she pushed them out again. Why should there be an enemy here?

The room was large and finely proportioned. There was a blue tea-set on the mantelpiece. Spode, bleu de roi, lovely and bright. It came to her then that she could recognize a sort of china, and yet she didn't know her own name. And she hadn't the slightest doubt about

166

the china — she knew it. Did that mean that she had lived with a set like that, known it intimately? She couldn't answer that at all.

She went on looking about the room. There were rugs on the floor — oriental rugs, small and good. They didn't touch each other, and the space between showed polished parquet. There were books — a great many books. There was a dear little walnut writing-table. And over the mantelpiece, where it reflected the blue china, there was a lovely walnut mirror.

She had got back to the mirror, when the door opened and Janet came in with a bowl of thick soup in her hand, Lizabet behind her with bread and butter. She had a rather wary expression. Her eyes darted at Anne and withdrew. At the sight of the food Anne realized how hungry she was. She had come out in the morning with nothing but a cup of tea. Everything in that house had tasted dirty, and the milk was sour. The soup smelled delicious. There was meat in it, and little suet balls. She took it all, Janet sitting beside her, talking just enough to make her feel at home. Lizabet had gone away, but she came back presently with the custard and the cheese. Every time she came into the room she looked at Anne in the same curious way. Anne thought she was like a spoiled child not accustomed to being crossed. She didn't want to cross her. She only wanted to find a room and to find work. It wouldn't do for her to come here and make trouble for Janet.

And then Lizabet was putting the custard pudding in front of her and saying in a curious pettish voice, "Janet says I have been rude. I'm sorry."

There was something touching about it. Anne found herself putting out her hand and saying, "Don't think of it. I'm not staying. Your cousin was so kind — but I'm not staying really."

Janet was behind her. She didn't move. Anne thought she looked upset, for Lizabet began to twist her fingers.

"You mustn't go away because of me. Janet will be so cross if you do." She was like a little girl. Anne wondered how old she was.

Janet came forward, and Lizabet ran out of the room. Janet said, "Don't take any notice of her. She's been spoilt. She's my cousin, you know, and she had her home with my grandfather. He let her do anything she liked. When he died she had to come to me. I can manage her, but not if everyone else gives in to her. Do you feel better? Would you like to see your room? It's one flight farther up. Lizabet's up there too. Yours is the other front room."

"But —" Anne checked herself, coloured, and said, "Who does the house belong to? Perhaps she won't like to take me."

"The house belongs to me. That is, it belonged to my parents. When they died, and everything got so expensive, I realized that something would have to be done. Our old cook Mrs Bingham took the basement. Her husband is a watchman in a jeweller's shop, so he's out all night. There are two girls on the top floor, you and Lizabet on the next, and an old lady on the two ground floors. I am in the back half of this room. Another cousin of mine has been in the room you are to have, but she went out yesterday. She doesn't like town, so she's going down into Dorset to keep chickens with a friend. A frightful life, I should say, but it takes all sorts to make the world, and she *hates* town. Funny, isn't it?"

It came on Anne that she didn't know whether it was funny or not. It came to her that she didn't know what her life had been. She put the tray down carefully and got up to follow Janet to the room she was to have.

CHAPTER
THIRTY-TWO

Jim Fancourt walked into Miss Silver's sitting-room. He could hardly wait for Emma Meadows to shut the door behind him, or for Miss Silver to shake hands, before he said, "I've been thinking —"

Miss Silver gave a faint reproving cough.

"Will you not sit down?"

"Thank you, I'd rather stand."

Miss Silver seated herself. She took her knitting-bag from the small table beside her chair and began to knit. Jim Fancourt stood before the hearth. When she had knitted about a row and a half, he came out with something between a groan and a cough.

"You haven't heard any more?"

Miss Silver was not prepared to tell an untruth. She said, "I have heard something, but not from Anne herself."

He had been turned half away from her, looking down into the fire. He was round in a flash.

"What do you mean?"

"Just what I said, Mr Fancourt. I have some news of Anne, but not from herself. I rang up your rooms, but you had already left. I felt sure that you would be very much relieved to have such satisfactory news."

170

He didn't know how dreadfully afraid he had been until she said that Anne was safe. He didn't know how much his face gave away. He had to hear it again, to have it underlined.

"Where is she?"

"I do not think that I can tell you that. She is with the cousin of a girl whom I was able to help — a very nice steady person. She is quite safe, Mr Fancourt. You may be perfectly sure of that."

"You won't tell me where she is?"

Miss Silver laid down her knitting.

"I can make allowances for your impatience, but I will ask you to consider the circumstances. At the present moment Anne's desire is to be left alone. She is perfectly safe, and you will do well to have regard to her wishes."

He bit his lip.

"That is all very well —"

"Yes, I think that it is. I think that you will achieve more by giving her a little time to, shall we say, miss you."

"Do you think she will?"

"I think so, if you do not alarm her by trying to force a decision upon her before she is prepared to make one."

"What decision do you mean?"

"Think for a minute, Mr Fancourt. Anne is not your wife — that has become quite clear."

"I never said she was."

"No. But with her memory gone, and in your absence, she was presented to your family in that light.

Then you arrived, and I suppose that was a shock to her."

"I suppose it was."

They were both talking so seriously that to neither of them did it seem at all strange that it should be put like that. Miss Silver leaned forward.

"Do you not see, Mr Fancourt, how it was? I do not know what your feelings were for the poor girl who was murdered. I do not know whether the form of marriage you went through with her would have held water. But all that is now beside the point. I think you must see that Anne will need a little time to think before any decision is taken as to your relationship. She is in the position of having no past. I do not think that she can decide upon her future until she knows what that past may have been. The best thing for her, and the thing most likely to clear up her thoughts, is a period of rest. What she needs is a time when nothing happens, a time in which she can feel secure and, if it works out that way, regain her memory."

"Yes — yes, I can see that. But she'll need money. Will you see that she has what she wants? I'll give you a cheque. Will fifty pounds be all right?"

"Yes, Mr Fancourt."

"Couldn't you tell me where she is?"

She smiled.

"I think it will be better if I do not."

He leaned forward and took her hands. His were hard and strong, but she felt them tremble.

"If I say I won't see her — I won't go near her —"

"Do you think you could really keep to that?"

He said, "I don't know. I suppose I couldn't, but I would try."

Miss Silver looked at him with a great degree of kindness. She said, "Let it alone for a little, Mr Fancourt. It will be better that way."

CHAPTER
THIRTY-THREE

Having let go, it is always difficult to take things up again. Anne had let go. She felt that way about it. It was as if she had been climbing a very steep hill, the sort of hill that it takes every atom of your strength to climb, and then quite suddenly she had come out upon a flat, easy place where she could stop and rest. A week went by. She did not know that a process of healing was going on. She did not see, as Janet saw, that there was a change in her — colour coming back to her cheeks and light to her eyes.

She woke up suddenly after a week to think about how much money she had. She came down to breakfast with a troubled look, and was glad to find Janet alone.

"I must get something to do."

"There's no hurry."

"Oh, but there is. I must get a job. I haven't much money."

Janet hesitated.

"You've got plenty for the present. I shouldn't be in a hurry."

Anne looked at her in a distressed way.

"You're so good to me. But don't you see I can't go on taking it? You don't know anything about me, and if you let a room you've a right to be paid for it, and — and I ought to be earning something."

Janet went on putting out the breakfast things. She didn't want to tell her, but she would have to. She hoped Anne wasn't going to mind. She said, "You needn't worry about the money."

Anne was looking at her with wide, distressed eyes.

"You're so good — but I must."

Janet stood there with the teapot in her hand.

"You know you spoke about Miss Silver — I told her you had come to me."

The blood ran up to the roots of Anne's hair and then down again. She looked as if she was going to faint. Janet put her in a chair and pulled up one beside her. She had been talking for some time before what she said came through to Anne.

"— fifty pounds. Have you got that? You don't look as if you had."

Anne said, "No — no —"

"Yes," said Janet firmly, "there's fifty pounds for you."

Anne came back slowly. Janet was sitting beside her, holding her hand.

"Miss Silver sent me fifty pounds, and it was for you."

The colour came into Anne's face again.

"He — he mustn't," she said.

"What do you mean?"

Anne's hand went out.

175

"It's from Jim. He mustn't —"

"Why?"

Anne was shaking.

"He — he mustn't. I don't want him to."

Janet was frowning.

"Look here, Anne, I do think you've got to be helped just now. Miss Silver says he's in a dreadful state about you."

"Is he?"

"She says he is. Look here, if Miss Silver says it's all right for you to take the money you really needn't worry. She's like all the maiden aunts in the world. If she says it's all right, then it is, and that's that."

"Does she say it's all right?"

"She wouldn't send it on if she didn't think so."

Anne woke up to the fact that she was talking about Jim, and — did Janet know anything about Jim? If she did, it wasn't Anne who had told her. Jim had been in her mind, in her thoughts, but she had never mentioned his name until now. She said, "Who told you about Jim?"

"Miss Silver thought I knew."

"You've seen her?"

"Yes, I have. That's when she gave me the money. She said it would be kind to take it because he was in such a state about you. You can pay it back, you know."

Anne said slowly, "Yes — I can pay it back —" And then Lizabet came in and there was no more private talk.

176

The letter from Jim came next morning. She didn't know it was from Jim at first, because it was enclosed in one from Miss Silver. She read Miss Silver's first.

My dear Anne,

I am very glad to have news of you, and to know that you are safe. Mr Fancourt has been in a great state about you. I have told him that he must wait until it is your wish to see him. Do not keep him too long, my dear. He is very much concerned for you, and quite trustworthy.

With affectionate regards,

Yours, Maud Silver.

Anne looked up from the neat handwriting to the enclosure, which wasn't neat at all. Something of the desperation in his mind came across to her as she looked at the envelope with the name that wasn't hers scrawled across it — Mrs Fancourt. That touched her. Suddenly and unexpectedly it touched her. She was trying to break away, and it was just as if he had put out a hand and caught at her to make her stay. She took the letter, ran up to her room with it, and locked the door. And even then she couldn't open it or read it for a long, long time. She wanted to, and she was afraid. She wanted to with all her heart, and just because she wanted to so much she was more afraid than she had ever been about anything.

When at last she moved, it was with a strong effort. She tore the envelope, and out came the package of sheets which were inside.

The letter began without any beginning as formal as beginnings go. It said:

Why did you go away like that? It was cruel of you and quite useless. Don't you know — don't you *know* that I care for you? You *must* know it. Let me come to you. I don't know why you went away. I think Lilian had something to do with it. You need never see her again if she had. I can promise you that. There is nothing else that I can think of that would come between us. Miss Silver says that you are safe. She won't tell me where you are. She says she only knows in confidence, and that she won't tell me unless you say she may. *Oh, Anne, please do say so — please.* Whatever is the matter — whatever you think you must keep to yourself, please, please, *please* let me know about it. I only want to help you. Darling — darling Anne, do believe that. You may feel that it is too soon for me to say all this. I know I shan't change. I won't worry you, I will promise that. But do let me see you. Don't shut yourself off from me like this. I can't stand it.

There was a big bold "Jim" scrawled across the bottom.

Anne read her letter through three times. Then she put up her hand to her eyes, found that they were wet, and got out a handkerchief to dry them with. She didn't know why Jim's letter should have made her cry, but it had. Then she saw that there was another sheet.

It had dropped on the bed beside her. She picked it up and read it:

I haven't told you about Anne. There isn't much to tell. I hardly knew her. She was with her father in the place where we were. Her mother was Russian, and she had been brought up out there. I don't know whether she was legitimate. I think perhaps she wasn't, because her father, Borrowdale, was in such a state about her when he was dying. He met with an accident and only lived a few hours. He asked me to marry Anne and look after her. I hadn't had a lot to do with women, but there was no one else so I said yes. There wasn't much time to think. He sent for the local priest — it was ten miles over very rough country — and he married us. The priest had been gone about an hour when the American plane came down. They got off again after a couple of hours, and they took Anne with them. It was a bit of a wangle, so don't talk about it. There have been difficulties about getting anyone away from Russia, especially if their nationality wasn't quite clear, so that American plane was just what was wanted. I thought it was the safest thing for her. But how she came to be murdered in London I don't know, or how you got mixed up in it. Let me come and see you. *Please* do.

It was an extraordinary story. How and why had she come into it? She didn't know at all. To think about it

179

was like pushing at darkness itself. At dense darkness. Memory didn't come back that way. If it came, it would come naturally — as naturally as she remembered getting up this morning, or what she did yesterday.

After what seemed like a long time she got up and washed her face. She couldn't make up her mind what to say to him. She would have to write to him. What did she say? It wasn't that she distrusted him, but he might distrust her. Suppose she told him just what had happened — how she had come down in the night and found Lilian talking to the man whose name she didn't know. Suppose he didn't believe her. Her heart beat hard at the thought. Why should he believe her? Lilian was his own kin. If it hadn't been for that, she could have trusted him, but — She tried to put herself in his place. A strange girl with no background at all telling the strangest tale about the people you had known always. How could you believe her? How could you believe anything she said?

She didn't know.

CHAPTER
THIRTY-FOUR

Jim Fancourt came down to breakfast after a night of tumultuous dreams. There was a little pile of letters, and he was sorting them through when he came on Anne's and dropped the others. She wrote as he had done, without a formal beginning and without a formal address. He read:

> I don't know what to say. You don't know anything about me. I don't know anything about myself. You have sent me some money. I don't know whether I ought to take it, but I am going to just for now, on the condition that you let me pay it back when I have got a job. You needn't worry about me at all. Miss Silver knows the girl I'm with, and nobody could be kinder. Please wait a little before you try and see me. I want to think things out. If I could only remember — but it's no use trying, it only makes everything confused.

He put his head in his hands and groaned. Why wouldn't she? Because she didn't trust him? Because she didn't want to be rushed? That hurt a little less than the other. But there wasn't a word to explain why she had gone off in the middle of the night. He went over the scene with her on the open slope of the hill. She had told him everything then. How did he know that? The answer came passionately. He did know it, but he didn't know how he knew it. He just knew that everything was all right between them then. Whatever had happened, whatever had gone wrong, had come afterwards. Something had happened. What was it? Something had happened to make her run away in the middle of the night from Lilian's house — from Lilian. That was it — Lilian had done something that had driven her away. Now, what had Lilian done?

That she was an idle, mischief-making woman, he had no doubt, but the idlest mischief-maker in the world needs something to start her off. It came to him then and suddenly that the man who had frightened Anne in the garden might be in on it. He had gone to the house first, and he had seen Lilian. What had passed between them, and was that their first meeting? He had no idea, but he meant to find out. He looked at his watch. He could catch the eleven o'clock for Haleycott.

Lilian was considerably surprised at his arrival. She had been congratulating herself on the way she had managed. Anne had gone. Jim had come and gone. The man whom she knew as Maxton had gone. There was nothing to bring any of them back again except Jim, who would naturally come down occasionally on a family visit which could have no particular significance, and which would be quite pleasant. She was all for keeping up pleasant relations with the family. What she

182

had not allowed for was his coming down again right on top of his other visit and in such an exceedingly overbearing and difficult frame of mind. He had refused curtly to come into the garden and see how the borders were progressing, and had opened the study door, shown her in, and shut it again, all in the most peremptory manner.

She said, "*Really*, Jim!" And then, "What is it? What have I done?"

"That is what I mean to know. Just what have you done?"

She went back to her "*Really*, Jim!" And then, in a tumble of words, "I don't know what you can possibly mean. I don't think you can be well. I don't know what this is all about."

"Don't you? Are you sure, Lilian? Are you quite sure you don't know?"

She was beginning to be frightened. What did he know? How could he possibly know anything at all? He couldn't — he didn't! She opened her eyes as wide as they would go and said, "I don't know what you're talking about. I can only suppose that you're not well, or — or that you've been drinking."

"No, I've not been drinking. There's nothing wrong with me, Lilian. You'd better make up your mind to it and tell the truth. Anne told me about the man who came down to see her. I know that he saw you first. It's really quite useless to try and deceive me. I've come here to get the truth, and I mean to get it."

He saw real terror in her eyes. Her hand went up to her throat.

183

"I don't know — what you mean —"

"Look here," he said, "something happened here in the middle of the night when Anne disappeared. It's no good your telling me you don't know anything about it. It's no good, I say."

Lilian did the best she knew for herself. She broke into sobs.

"Really, Jim . . . I can't think . . . I don't know why! Oh — oh dear! What do you think I've done?"

He said, "I don't know. You'd better tell me. That man who came down — I want to know whether you had ever seen him before."

He didn't know, then. He wanted to know. Well, she wasn't going to tell him, and that would serve him right.

There was a sofa by the window. She made her way to it and sat down, moving feebly. It would serve him right if she were to faint. She wondered what he would do if she did, and then decided regretfully that she had better not. And it was quite obvious that he didn't know anything. He didn't *know* that she knew Maxton, or that Maxton had been here in the night. She must remember that he didn't know, and she must stick to it. She got out her handkerchief and dried her eyes.

"I don't know what this is all about," she said in the most pathetic voice she could contrive. "Anne ran away from here. I've no idea why, but if you want to know what I think —" She paused, mopped her eyes, and looked at him round the handkerchief. "If you want to know what I really think — well, I don't like to say it, but I've no doubt in my own mind —"

184

"What have you got no doubt about in your own mind?"

She wished that Jim would stay farther off. She wished she had not sat down, but her legs were shaking and she had to. She was afraid to say what she had begun to say, but there didn't seem to be any way out of it now. She spoke in rising agitation.

"I thought she was odd when she came — very odd. And I didn't think —" She stopped.

Jim repeated her last words. "You didn't think —"

Lilian was goaded into speech.

"I didn't think she was right in her head," she said.

CHAPTER
THIRTY-FIVE

Anne put on her hat and went out. She must think, and to think she must keep moving. When she sat still her thoughts were all confused. It was a clear, sunny afternoon. There was a blue sky deepening a little into mist, greying a little. There was no cloud, no cloud at all. The houses stood up tall and stiff. She wasn't thinking about what she had come out to think of. It was no good trying to think of things you had forgotten — thoughts just drifted . . . just drifted. It wasn't any use trying to remember. She knew that — she did know it really. Some day it would come again, the whole thing — who she was — what had happened to her — how she had come to the house with a dead girl in it. The curtain would lift quite suddenly and she would know it all. It wouldn't come with trying. It was no use to try — no use at all.

She walked on, not knowing where she was going. The air was pleasant, soft, and mild. It reminded her of something, she didn't know what — something very far back. And then suddenly she remembered. Only it wasn't autumn, it was spring — a spring day with the birds singing, and the sort of uprush of living that the spring gives you — or used to give you in the days when you were yourself and you knew who you were.

The spring — everything fresh and green. Aunt Letty always said the spring was the time for children and all the young things in the world. She remembered her quoting a piece out of the Bible about it . . . something about the singing of birds . . . and she said — she said — No, it was gone. She couldn't remember what Aunt Letty had said about spring.

Aunt Letty — who was Aunt Letty? She didn't know any more. She had been a child for a moment. Aunt Letty had been someone whom the child knew — knew very well. But it was gone again. She wasn't a child any more. It had all gone. Aunt — Aunt — she couldn't remember the name any more, it was all quite gone. Like something that had happened in another world, another life.

But it was her life, her very own life. She had nothing to put in the place of it, nothing at all, until she came to what was for her the dreadful beginning of her present experience — the dark stair — herself sitting crouched upon it, knowing that below her in the black dark a dead girl lay.

She stood still, shuddering violently, and stamped her foot. Had she no sense at all? Couldn't she control her thoughts better than this? The answer was that she hadn't been trying to control them. She had just been letting them drift, and that she mustn't do. Not ever.

For the first time she looked about her. She had been walking on, letting her thoughts run, not noticing where she was going. When there had been a crossing she had taken it mechanically. The thoughts that occupied her mind had given way and then closed in again. She had not noticed which way she went, only come out of her thoughts sufficiently to cross, to turn, to follow some road, some pattern that lay deep in her mind, too deep for conscious thought. Now, quite suddenly, she looked about her and saw a quiet decorous street and close beside her an entrance. She stood and looked at it.

Thoughts came up in her mind. She felt an extraordinary impulse to go in at the door. She even had a picture in her mind of the hall beyond. For the moment she could see it. The place was an hotel. There was a counter, and a girl who took your name down. She had a prompting to go in, to go up the stairs. And suddenly, quick on that, a flood of opposite thoughts, so strong that there was no escaping them. They turned her, set her feet going, so that she was walking hard, walking away with a most dreadful feeling of fear. She didn't know where it came from. She only knew that it took all her firmness, all her self-control, just to keep walking steadily as if she knew where she was going. There was no clue as to why she should feel as she did. It was just fear made manifest, and she didn't know why. She didn't know that she had just missed a meeting with Maxton, who had called at the Hood to enquire whether Miss Anne Forest had returned to the hotel. If she had gone up the steps and entered the hall of the Hood she would have met him face to face.

She walked on. She didn't know what an escape had been hers, but she felt a sense of relief, of release. She began to notice the faint sunshine, the light breeze. Her thoughts quieted. She began to think of Jim. He hadn't just rushed off and been glad to be rid of her. He really cared what happened to her — he really did care.

She walked quite a long way and thought about Jim.

CHAPTER
THIRTY-SIX

Anne got home just as it was getting dark. Janet looked up with a smile and said, "Here you are," in a voice from which she tried to banish the relief.

"I'm not late?"

"Oh, no — no."

Lizabet turned a page of her book and said, "Janet *thought* you had gone for ever. I didn't."

No one asked her why she didn't think so. When she had waited for a little she tossed her bright head and said languidly, "No such luck."

Anne had come in in such a state of contentment that she could laugh. She said, "Just wait a little, Lizabet."

When Anne went out of the room Janet followed her.

"She's like a child. It's very good of you not to mind. She's just a jealous child. I can't give way to her."

"No, I suppose not. I won't stay here. It makes things too uncomfortable for you."

"No — no, really! Lizabet must learn. She mustn't think she's the only one to be considered. That's bad for her. Very bad."

Anne made a little face.

"I don't know that I care about being a moral lesson."

They both laughed.

"Anne, I don't know what you'll say to this, but if you really do want to earn something —"

"Oh, yes, I do — I really do."

"Well then, I've had a call from my old cousin, Miss Carstairs. She lives in Devonshire, and she comes up to town once in a while and stays with an old maid of hers who lets rooms. I won't pretend she's easy to get on with — she's not. If you could stand it, she'd pay about three pounds a week, and the maid, Mrs Bobbett, lives just round the corner, so you wouldn't have to go wandering about."

"Could I do it? What would she want me to do?"

Janet laughed.

"I don't know. She has a friend, and the friend's got a family. Twice a year she goes off and sees them. It's a law of the Medes and Persians, and everything has to give way to it. Well, then Cousin Clarry comes up to town full of wrath and demandings. It isn't an easy time for anyone, and quite candidly it wouldn't be an easy time for you. I haven't said anything about it. For one thing, I didn't know just when she was coming, and for another, I really hadn't the nerve."

"You mean — Oh, Janet, how nice of you! You wouldn't say anything as long as you thought I couldn't very well refuse, only now — now that I'm not obliged to do it if I don't want to — Why, Janet, of course I will!"

"It will only be for a couple of weeks, and if you can't stand it —"

"You can stand anything for a couple of weeks," said Anne.

"Well, if you're sure — if you're quite sure —"

"Of course I am!"

It was all fixed up by telephone, Anne's part in the fixing being a silent one. She stood and heard Janet talk into the telephone.

"I have a friend, Cousin Clarry, who I think would be just the thing for you. She's staying here . . . Yes, with me. I think she is just what you are looking for." She paused. The telephone crackled vigorously. Miss Carstairs evidently had the gift of words. They poured out for about five minutes, after which time it became just possible to get in a word edgeways. Janet, apparently used to it, waited patiently. When the voice stopped for a moment, she resumed with calm.

"If you would care to see her, I could bring her round tomorrow morning, and if you thought she would do she could stay on for the rest of the day and come back here at night . . . Yes, three pounds a week will be all right. She's staying here, so it will be quite convenient . . . All right, I'll bring her round in the morning . . . Ten o'clock? . . . Goodbye." She hung up and turned round.

"Well, that's fixed. If you find you can't stick it you will just have to say so. Ten to six every day."

In both their minds was the unspoken thought that Anne would be out of Lizabet's way for the greater part of each day, and that would be something to the good.

Next morning Janet and Anne went through the square at a quarter to ten, turned to the left, and came up the next street, where the houses were a little shabbier but otherwise very much the same as in the square.

At the fifth house they stopped and rang the bell. A stout comfortable woman opened the door, beamed on Janet, and said, "Come up then, come up. She's all in a fidget. Wants to get settled like. Wants to see the young lady. Puts herself about like because she didn't think to say come round last night and fix it up. Never knew anyone worry herself like Miss Carstairs — never in my life!"

They were going up the stairs whilst she talked. When they came to what Mrs Bobbett called the first floor front she opened the door, said in a loud cheerful voice, "Miss Janet and the other young lady," and having shown them in disappeared from view and shut the door.

Miss Carstairs remained seated until they were half-way across the room. Then she got up and stood leaning on a black crooked stick and looking so exactly like an illustration in an old-fashioned book of fairy stories that Anne could hardly believe her eyes. She was the exact image of the Wicked Fairy who had terrorized her childish dreams. To begin with, she was only four foot eight or nine. It was a child's stature but not a childish face. The cheeks were pendulous and the nose curved. The eyes were very keen and black. And black too was the elaborately dressed hair — coal black without a grey hair to soften it. It lay above the peering brow in elaborate folds and scallops, tight, neat, and extraordinarily artificial. She wore a curious black velvet garment pinned in front with an elaborate and apparently very valuable diamond brooch. She stood there leaning on her stick and waited for them to come to her.

Janet bent and kissed one of the yellow cheeks. The embrace was received without any return. It was endured, not reciprocated. The little creature received it, waited for it to be over, and went on waiting.

Janet, a little flushed, introduced Anne.

"This is my friend whom I spoke to you about."

Miss Carstairs spoke. She had a deep, decided voice.

"You didn't tell me her name. Very careless, very careless indeed."

"Oh, she's Anne Fancourt," said Janet in a hurry.

Miss Carstairs did not offer to shake hands with Anne. She looked her up and down. Under that sharp gaze Anne felt herself looked through and through. There was something very unpleasant about the look. It seemed to say, "Hide from me and I'll find you. Oh, yes, I'll find you, no matter how clever you think yourself."

Where Janet had coloured, Anne turned pale. And then the moment was over. The sharp black eyes shifted, the stick on which the little figure leaned moved. Miss Carstairs went back a step, seated herself, and leaning forward still propped on her stick, addressed Janet.

"She understands what I want?"

Anne answered her.

194

"You want someone to be useful to you — to take the place of your companion whilst she is on holiday."

Miss Carstairs gave her a sharp look.

"Not much holiday about it if the truth were told. Ada Lushington is a born fool to go near her cousin. The most disagreeable woman I ever saw in my life, and just because she's taken to her bed there's Ada gone pounding off on what she calls a holiday to see her! Holiday indeed!" She laughed angrily. "But there, Ada's a fool, and that's all there is to it! Goodbye, Janet — I needn't keep you. You'll have plenty to do looking after that cousin of yours — what's her name?"

"Do you mean Lizabet?"

"Who? No, I don't mean anything of the sort. *Lizabet indeed!* Why, I was at the christening myself, and the name she was given was Elizabeth. You can bring her round at tea-time tomorrow. Get along on with you!"

Janet got along on. She had really forgotten how impossible Cousin Clarry could be — or else she had got worse. She ought never to have exposed Anne to this. Oh, well, there was nothing she could do about it now. She went down the stairs, stopping at the turn for a moment and hearing Cousin Clarry's harsh, deep voice take up the talk.

CHAPTER
THIRTY-SEVEN

The first thing that Miss Carstairs said when they were left alone was a challenge to Anne's self-possession. She sat there, her hands crossed on the crutch of her stick and her head on one side.

"Well?" she said. "What do you make of me? Do I eat the young, or don't I?"

Anne found herself laughing.

"I don't think you do."

"Oh, well, if I try you can always walk out, can't you? How do you get on with Elizabeth? And don't pretend you don't know who I mean — but call her Lizabet I will not. It's not her name, and that's all there is to it."

"Was she christened Elizabeth?"

"She was. And what's wrong with that, I ask you. Lizabet's rubbish! When she comes here she gets her Christian name, and that's Elizabeth, after my poor cousin that was her mother. You didn't know her?"

"No."

She got a sharp glance.

"I never heard of you in my life till last night when Janet answered my call. How long have you known her?"

"Not very long."

"I never heard of you before. Don't stand there towering over me! Take off your hat and your gloves and sit down! There — that's better. What were we talking about?"

"I don't know."

"You're not half-witted, are you? Of course you know! We were talking about Elizabeth. Janet got herself fairly tied up with that young woman. She'll be sorry before she's through with it. But she won't listen, of course. She knows best, and she'll go on knowing best until that Elizabeth girl has dragged her into some mess or other. And when she has, she'll expect me not to say 'I told you so'! And she may expect! Now, how do you come into it all? You might as well answer me truthfully, for I shall go on asking you until you do."

It came into Anne's mind that she was speaking the truth, and that there were only two ways of it — either she joined the truth-telling party, or she didn't. If she didn't she could get up and say goodbye and walk out. All right, which was it to be? It was her choice. And quite suddenly she knew what she would do. All right, she wanted to know — well then, let her know and see what she made of it. She leaned forward a little and said as if it was the most natural thing in the world, "I've lost my memory."

"You've *what*?"

"I've lost my memory. I don't know who I am, or what my name is."

Miss Carstairs thumped with her stick. Her black eyes stared.

"Go on — tell me!"

Anne smiled at her.

"But that's all."

"Nonsense — it can't be! Doesn't Janet know who you are?"

"No, she doesn't."

"Have you been to the police?"

"No — I don't want to."

"Why don't you want to?"

"I don't know."

"Anyone would say that was a bad sign. I don't know that I would myself. Go to the police and you go to the papers, that's what I say. And of course that's just what they want, most of these people who say they've lost their memory — only want to get into the papers and make a splash." Her eyes went over Anne in a queer bright look. "No, you're not like that. You haven't told me everything, have you?"

"No, not everything."

"No tarradiddles?"

"No — I wouldn't do that."

"H'm." The black eyes looked very straight at Anne. They went on looking for a long time. In the end she said "H'm" again and got up.

"Come into the other room and unpack for me," she said, and led the way.

Her bedroom was at the back of the house. It was untidy to the last degree. There were shawls, a dressing-gown, skirts, underclothes, all tossed, some on the bed, some on the floor. As Anne went about the business of picking them up and sorting them out, Miss Carstairs watched her from a seat on the bed. She took the same position as she had done in the chair, leaning forward with her hands on the stick, her chin propped on the handle, her eyes very bright and attentive. And all the while she talked.

"Ada's the worst packer in the world. The dresses will all have to hang, and one must just hope that the creases will come out. If Janet had had the sense to send you round yesterday it wouldn't have been such a business. We must just hope for the best. Ever done anything like this before?"

"Yes — I think so —"

"But you don't know if it was for yourself, or for someone else?"

"I think it was for myself."

"What makes you think that?"

"I don't know — I think —"

"Well, what do you think?"

Anne stood in the middle of the floor, but she wasn't really there. She was packing a blue and silver dress. She saw it quite clearly for a moment. It was a lovely dress. The feel of it was in her hands, and then it was gone again. What she had in her hands was not blue and silver but black and gold — stiff black brocade with a gold pattern on it. Across the black and gold, black eyes were looking at her, searching, full of interest.

"Well, what did you see?"

She had no thought but to answer truthfully.

"I saw a blue and silver dress. I think it was mine."

Miss Carstairs broke into harsh laughter.

"Blue and silver? That would be pretty. And it would suit you — oh, yes, quite. You didn't have it on, did you?"

"No, I was lifting it —" Her voice failed suddenly.

"H'm. Often do that sort of thing?"

"No, I don't."

"Oh, well, you had a blue and silver dress, and you've remembered it. There's nothing so extraordinary about that. By and by you'll remember everything. But don't chase after it — that's fatal. When it comes it will come — just like that, without any effort. But if you try for it, the mist will thicken and you'll get nowhere at all." She nodded her head and said in a different voice, "That's enough about that. Just get on with the unpacking."

CHAPTER
THIRTY-EIGHT

They got on with the unpacking, and when everything was neatly arranged Miss Carstairs put on a very handsome fur coat and a bonnet of black velvet with a wonderful steel ornament on one side, called for a cab, and took her way to the shops. She had pale grey gloves and pale grey shoes which she told Anne were only "ones". She seemed very proud of this, and explained that she had them specially made for her as there was no demand for the size in a grown-up shoe. She seemed to be pleased with Anne's society.

"Ada is nothing but a wet fish," she explained. "Of course she hasn't any money, so she can't spend any. It makes her the most tiresome company you can imagine on a shopping expedition. Quality means nothing to her — nothing at all. Cheapness is her one criterion of value, and the result is that I invariably spend at least twice as much as I mean to when I go shopping with her. Now you can urge me on, and when I'm urged on, the natural reaction is to draw back. Do you understand that?"

The question was so sharply put that it startled Anne. She coloured brightly and said, "No — yes —" And then, "I think I do."

They embarked on an orgy of shopping. Miss Carstairs wished to buy a carpet for her bedroom and stuff for curtains.

"Twenty years I've had the old ones," she told the middle-aged man who served them. "Twenty years, and the stuff's not worn out yet. It will do very nicely for my companion, and she'll feel easier with that than she would with everything new, which she'd just think of as gross extravagance and be haunted in her dreams. I'm going to get a new carpet too, and she can have my old one. She's too poor-spirited to enjoy a new one. As it is, she'll be worrying over mine being too fine for me." She broke into deep laughter.

The man who was serving them thought to himself that she wouldn't be the easiest person to be a companion to. He didn't know if it was the young lady with her that she was talking about. If it was, he was sorry for her, for she hadn't got an easy job — not an easy job at all. His feelings became intensified as he got out roll upon roll of flowered chintz, each fresh piece being greeted with "That's very nice, that's very nice indeed, but I'll just see what else you have if you don't mind."

In the end she had selected six pieces, all of which she praised, but none of which could she decide upon, when, suddenly weary of her pastime, she chose a flowery affair with a pattern of foxgloves, and then proceeded to the acquisition of a plain dull purple for the carpet.

It was when they were leaving the department that they saw the young man in a grey suit. Miss Carstairs had given her address and detailed instructions as to the day on which the carpet and the stuff for curtains were to be sent off.

She had written a cheque, and the shopman was congratulating himself upon having done a useful morning's work, when the good-looking young man crossed their path. He did not see them, his attention being taken up with the people he was with. Miss Carstairs looked at him across the room and gave a deep chuckle.

"That's funny," she said, "that's very funny indeed."

Since she was obviously expected to comment, Anne did so. She asked, "What is amusing you?" and received a reply which told her nothing.

"Oh, ho, ho — it's very funny indeed if you know what I know! But you don't! No, my dear, you don't — you don't know anything at all!"

Anne laughed, because the tone was good-tempered. She laughed, and she looked where Miss Carstairs was looking and she nearly dropped, because she knew the face of the young man in grey. Just for a moment she knew him. Who he was, and what he had to do with her. Her head whirled. She put out her hand and it touched the counter — something strong and firm to lean against. She leaned there, and for a moment everything swung round her. Then her head cleared, her eyes saw. Everything round her was quiet, and the man in the grey suit wasn't there. Miss Carstairs was looking in the direction where he had been. She had apparently not noticed Anne's sudden faintness. She said, "That's a young man who didn't know which side his bread was buttered."

"What's his name?"

"I don't know. I suppose I did know, but I've forgotten . . . Craddock — Crockett — oh, I can't tell you, but it doesn't matter."

"Do you know the people he was with?"

She oughtn't to have gone on about it. Her voice wasn't steady enough. She got one of those direct looks which seemed to walk in amongst her thoughts and take stock of them no matter whether the door was locked or not. She had a sense of ruthless enquiry.

The deep, rather harsh voice rang in her ears. "No, I don't. Do you?"

The words were not loud, but they buffeted her. She said, "No," and thought how unconvincing it sounded.

"You don't know them?"

"No, I don't." This time she made herself meet the hard black eyes. She saw them snap.

"Well, you nearly faint when you see some very ordinary people at the end of a room. If it wasn't the women who upset you, then it was the man. What about it?"

Anne felt as if she knew nothing — not who she was, or why, or anything. She said, "I don't know."

Miss Carstairs gave her a look and began to talk about Ada Lushington — her likes, her dislikes, her extraordinary fondness for cats.

"She'd have a dozen if I let her. As it is, we have four, and that's three too many. I've no objection to one cat provided it's healthy and not the sort that goes on

204

having kittens whether one wants them or not. But four! I've told Ada that it's three too many, and that she's got to find homes for the others, or else some day she'll come in and find there are three cats missing. And what do you think she had the nerve to say to me? You'll not guess, I assure you. She had the impudence to say that I was fond of the creatures myself, and that if I found homes for them they would be very good ones. Now what do you say to that?"

The young man in the grey suit was gone. He was wiped clear from Anne's mind. She remembered seeing him, but she couldn't think why it had upset her. She had never seen him before. She was sure about that. Well then, what was there to worry about? Nothing — or everything in the world —

The deep places that were under her thought stirred and were moved. She came back with a shudder and listened to Miss Carstairs, who was looking at her enquiringly and asking in a very determined voice, "Now what do you say to that?"

The colour came into her face with a rush. She said in an eager, fluttering voice, "I think she was right."

Miss Carstairs was very much taken aback.

"Oh, you do, do you?" She stared for a long protesting minute, and then said sharply, "I don't believe you heard what I said. Not that it was worth hearing anyway. And now I have to get some ribbon for garters. Can you make garters?"

"I think so."

"You must know if you can. I like my garters smart. We'll get the ribbon for them this morning, and you can make them this afternoon. We shall want elastic too. I can give you a pair to copy."

Outside the shop Ross Cranston said goodbye to his friends, who were Mrs Magstock and her sister-in-law Sylvia. He had met them quite by chance, and they had disturbed his mind. Sylvia Magstock was quite a pretty girl, and she was willing enough. The meeting had been a chance one, but he could easily arrange that there should be others. He knew where they were staying — he could ring up later in the day. If only — if only . . . a sense of having gone too far to draw back came into his mind. It was like seeing something horrible a long way off and knowing that every step you took brought you nearer to it. He shuddered violently, and the picture grew more distinct. It was what he always tried not to remember and found it so difficult to forget — the picture of a girl lying dead at the foot of a dark underground stair.

He shook it violently from his mind and went on his way.

CHAPTER
THIRTY-NINE

Anne got home at half-past six. When she had taken off her things she came downstairs, to find Lizabet and no Janet. She had gone out to see a friend who had been ill.

"And if you ask me, I think she's an idiot to put herself about for people like she does. If you start propping people up you can just go on and they get worse instead of better — that's what I think. But I suppose you approve."

"Why do you suppose that?"

"I wonder why —" Lizabet had a book on her lap, but she wasn't reading. "Oh, just what's sauce for the goose might be supposed to be sauce for the — oh, but I mustn't say that, or you'll tattle to Janet, and then I shall get into a row, and you'd like that, wouldn't you?"

Anne came back from a long way off. She said steadily, "Look here, Lizabet, you don't like me, and you don't like my being here. Well, I'm not going to stay, so you needn't bother."

Lizabet screwed up her face.

"Sez you!"

Anne kept her temper.

"Well, I'm the one who knows. You don't like me, but I take it you do like Janet — you're fond of her. Couldn't you put up with me for a bit just to please her? I'm looking for a job."

"You've got one."

"It's not permanent. You must know that. It's just for the fortnight Miss Lushington will be away. There won't be any opportunity of our seeing much of each other."

"Only in the evenings," said Lizabet with a toss of the head. "And every morning before you go. It makes me sick to see Janet waiting on you!"

"She doesn't."

Lizabet tossed her head.

"You wouldn't notice of course!"

Janet came in just before seven.

"Poor Magda," she said, "she's in the most dreadful dumps."

"And of course she's got to unload them on you!" said Lizabet.

Janet coloured.

"Oh, well," she said in a placatory voice. Then she laughed. "I didn't mean to bring it home with me."

Still without looking up from her book, Lizabet was heard to murmur, "You do rather bring them home with you, darling, don't you?"

In the morning Anne went back to Miss Carstairs. The evening had convinced her that she must find somewhere else to live. She would talk to Janet about it. Lizabet was tiresome, and it was no good trying to alter her. Talking to her only made her worse. She was quite convinced that she meant mischief of some sort, and everything that she said or did added to this conviction. It's no good struggling with that sort of thing, you must just keep clear of it, or as clear of it as you can. She wasn't prepared to give up her friendship with Janet, but there was no need for it to be under Lizabet's observation. By the time she reached Miss Carstairs' rooms she had the whole thing nicely settled in her mind.

When Mrs Bobbett opened the door to her, she made her enquiry.

"Mrs Bobbett, do you know of anything that would suit me? I'm afraid I can't pay very much, but I'd do my own room, and I'd be very willing to help in any other way I could."

Mrs Bobbett stood still on the stairs and thought.

"What sort of room do you want?"

"Oh, just somewhere to sleep. You see, I don't know quite what I'm going to do yet, and I mustn't spend too much. I just want to be sure that it's all right."

Mrs Bobbett looked down and looked up again.

"There's a room upstairs you could have. It's small and the roof slopes, and I don't generally let it and that's the truth. Sort of a spare room, that's what it is. I'm next door myself, and when my niece comes up from the country I put her there. If you'd like to see it —"

The room was small, but exquisitely tidy and clean. Anne told Mrs Bobbett that she would take it, and went down to Miss Carstairs with a feeling of exhilaration which dropped suddenly from a full peak of almost breathless confidence into a vague feeling of distress. She didn't know what it was, or where it came from. It wasn't like her at all, but she couldn't shake it off. It stayed with her and tinged the day with foreboding.

She told herself it was the weather. They were all ready to go out, when the rain came down and Miss Carstairs said crossly that she never went out when it was raining.

"I don't know why we put up with this climate at all! I should think when they're always inventing things they might just as well do something about the weather! Rain so many days, and at night, instead of in the morning when one wants to go out and do things!"

"Everybody would want something different," said Anne. "People who were going out in the evening wouldn't want it to be wet then. And who would decide when it was to rain? Nothing they did would suit everyone, and the people it didn't suit would get up societies, and processions, and meetings."

"Well, that would be something to do, wouldn't it?" said Miss Carstairs crossly. Then she made a face and burst out laughing. "You know, I hate to be dull. When I'm at home I can do all sorts of things — turn out old letters, old photographs. There's a lot in doing that. You can make the past live again, and some of it wasn't too bad. But when I'm away from home I expect to go about and enjoy myself. And frankly, it's a relief getting rid of Ada — for a bit anyhow. I wouldn't like to feel I wasn't going to see her again or anything like that, but there are times when I can do without her. And my

210

conscience doesn't bother me when she's gone on her own affairs. Perhaps you didn't think I'd got a conscience, but I have."

It cleared up after lunch, and they went out. Anne, urged by Miss Carstairs, bought the stuff for two nightgowns.

CHAPTER
FORTY

Lizabet looked into the sitting-room and saw Anne there alone. She came in, shut the door after her, and sat down on the arm of a chair a little to one side of Anne. Anne had cut out the two nightgowns and was sewing on a long pink seam. She looked up when Lizabet came in and waited for her to speak. Lizabet looked her over, but she didn't speak. Anne felt herself colouring. She looked down at her work and went on sewing. As soon as she looked away Lizabet said, "How long are you going to stay here?"

Anne looked up.

"I don't know."

"Hadn't you better think about it?"

Anne put her work down and looked at her.

"You don't like my being here."

Lizabet tossed her head.

"Isn't that funny of me!"

"I think it is rather. Why do you mind?"

Lizabet put her hands down on the arm of the chair and leaned forward.

"Who are you? Where do you come from? Why are you hiding?"

"I'm not hiding."

Lizabet tossed her head.

"Oh, yes, you are. Janet says not to talk about your being here — not to anyone. Why does she do that if you haven't got something to hide? Something horrid! And I won't have it! I won't have you dragging Janet into whatever you're mixed up in! And it's no use telling me you're not mixed up in anything, because I wouldn't believe you! Do you hear — I wouldn't believe you!"

What does one say to an unreasonable jealous child? Anne didn't know. For Janet's sake she would do what she could. She said, "You are making it very difficult, you know."

"I am making it difficult?"

"Well, you're not making it easy. I'm sorry you don't like my being here. It will only be for a little while."

Lizabet tossed her head.

"Am I expected to like it?"

Anne was divided between a desire to laugh and a desire to cry. She managed the laugh, but it was rather a shaky one.

"Lizabet, don't be so difficult. Can't you put up with me for a week or two?"

"If it were really only for a week or two —"

"It won't be for longer. I'll promise you that, if you like."

Lizabet coloured suddenly, deeply. She stamped with her foot.

"Do you think I believe anything you say? Well then, I don't — I don't — I don't!"

As she reached the second "don't", they both heard the front door close on the floor below. Lizabet swung round and ran out of the room. Anne could hear her running up to the next floor and banging her door. She herself was shaking all over. She would have to get out as soon as she could. Lizabet was a spoilt child. But Janet — it wasn't fair to Janet. She must get away as soon as she decently could.

Janet had been to see Miss Silver. She went because she wanted to talk about Anne. Did Miss Silver think that Jim Fancourt was really in earnest and really to be trusted?

Miss Silver did. And gave her reasons. Having got so far, Janet hesitated, and then came out with, "I'm having a very difficult time with my cousin. She has been thoroughly spoilt . . . Oh, not by me. She hasn't been with me for very long, but she's been very difficult. You see, she's been the first object of consideration both with her grandfather and with her old nurse, and she's jealous. She's only seventeen. It's not Anne's fault at all. She has done everything she can to make friends with her, but Lizabet simply won't. And I wondered —" She stopped and fixed her distressed eyes on Miss Silver.

"What did you wonder, my dear?"

Janet said, "I don't know. It's not like me to be uncertain about what I should do, but I am. Lizabet is so young and she's been so spoilt, she might do anything. But if it's only for a little time, I can manage her, I think."

She came away a good deal relieved and encouraged. Miss Silver did not think that she would need to be responsible for Anne for very long. She thought that there would be developments soon, and anyhow she was convinced that she could find suitable accommodation for her.

"It might be better if she were near you without being under the same roof. You could go and see her without rousing up this tiresome jealousy on your cousin's part."

Janet returned home much encouraged. She was a great deal too much taken up with her thoughts to notice the man who had been hanging about in the street opposite Miss Silver's, and who turned and followed her when she left.

CHAPTER
FORTY-ONE

Lizabet was looking out of her window. She was full of jealousy and anger and spite. Janet had come into the house, but she hadn't come to look for her. She had gone into the sitting-room, and there she was, talking to Anne. Before Anne came to them it was Lizabet whom she would have called out for the moment she came in. Now she went straight into the sitting-room and stayed there talking to Anne! She stamped her foot so hard that it hurt, and stared out at the quiet street.

There was a man there. He was looking at the numbers. Presently he turned away and crossed over. Lizabet had the strangest idea that he had been on the point of ringing their bell and had thought better of it. She picked up a hat and ran lightly down the stairs. If Janet came out of the sitting-room, she could say she was going to the post. But Janet didn't come out. They were much too busy talking to know, or to care, that she had come down. A sharp little jab of anger caught her as she opened the front door and looked up the road.

The man was about half-way to the corner. She needn't speak to him. She could catch him up easily enough without his noticing. She could just walk past him and go up to the pillar-box at the corner and pretend to be posting something, and that would give her a good opportunity of looking at him. If she liked him, she would say something. If she didn't like him, there was no harm done.

She quickened her steps, came up with the man, who was walking slowly, passed him, and came to the pillar-box. There she went through the pretence of posting a letter and allowed her eyes to rest on the man whom she had passed. She thought him very good-looking. He wasn't the man whom Anne had seen at Chantreys. He was younger and much better-looking. When he saw Lizabet staring at him he smiled and took off his hat.

"I wonder if you could tell me what street this is?"

Lizabet coloured brightly. She had only been long enough in London to think Janet was very un-up-to-date. When you have lived in a village all your life and been the squire's granddaughter, and when everyone knows you and has known you since you were in your cradle, it gives you a certain feeling of confidence. This had, unfortunately, not had time to wear off. Janet had preached, but of course Lizabet knew better. She responded in the friendliest manner.

"Can I help you?"

"I just wondered whether you knew a friend of mine who I believe lives near here. It's so very awkward not having her address. I suppose you can't help me?"

"I don't know."

She wouldn't have thought anything of a stranger asking a question of that sort in Cruxford, so why should she think anything of it here? But all the time something niggled at her. She knew very well what Janet would say. Janet was old-fashioned and pernickety. Janet wasn't treating her properly — coming into the house like that and not so much as calling out to know if she was there! Other people thought her worth noticing. This young man did. She pushed the feeling about not speaking to strangers right into the back of her mind.

The man spared an admiring thought from his preoccupation. This was a very pretty girl, and she was very young — seventeen — eighteen perhaps? He was in luck. He let a respectful admiration appear and said, "Her name is Anne —"

He noted her reaction. She knew Anne. He said, "I didn't say her surname. There was some talk of her being married, but I don't know if it was true. I must know."

"Anne Fancourt?"

"Oh, you do know her?"

"I know Anne Fancourt."

All at once she was a little frightened. She remembered Janet, and what Janet would say about talking to a strange man whom she had met in the street. She coloured suddenly and vividly.

"I — I don't think I ought to go on talking about her. I — I don't think she'd like it."

"Perhaps she wouldn't. But then again, perhaps she would. I've been looking for her for a long time. Perhaps she'll be very pleased to be found."

"Do you think she would?"

218

"She might be. One can but try. Only —" He hesitated. "Will you do something to help me?"

"If I can."

"Well, don't tell her you've seen me. I'd like it to be a surprise. The fact is we quarrelled, and if you say you've met me, she'll go all hard and stiff and say she won't see me. You know how girls are. If she wasn't expecting me it would be different. She wouldn't have time to remember our quarrel or to stiffen herself up against me. You know how it is?"

Lizabet nodded. She knew just how it was. She felt wise and benevolent. She would bring Anne and this young man together, and then Anne would go away with him, and she and Janet could go back comfortably to their own way of life. Everything had been all right before Anne came. Everything would be all right when she had gone away. This young man knew who she was and he would take her away. Nothing could be simpler. She spoke quickly. "Oh, yes — I'd like to help! What shall I do?"

Ross Cranston considered. He said, "Wait a minute —" And then, "Could you — do you think you could get her to come out of the house to post a letter or something of that kind?"

"Oh, yes, I think I could. I could try."

"You see, if I came to the house, she might say she wouldn't see me. I can't risk that. But if she goes out to post a letter and I come up just as she's got to the pillar-box, it would give me a chance, wouldn't it? You see, I must know whether she's married or not. If she is, I'll go away, but if she isn't —"

"Oh, yes!"

Lizabet's eyes were dancing. This was a lovely plan. She would be rid of Anne, and she wouldn't be doing anyone any harm. Nobody could say there was a scrap of harm in it. She would be restoring Anne to her friends and relations, and she would be getting rid of her. It was a *lovely* plan. She beamed at Ross Cranston, and when he said, "Then it's a bargain," and held out his hand she put hers into it and felt very pleased with herself.

It wasn't really as difficult as it might have been. She got home, and then she sat down and wrote a letter. It didn't really matter to whom. Nanna would do . . . yes, Nanna would do very well. And then she only had to act a little, and she quite enjoyed that.

The first thing to do was to let Janet go off to bed, and fortunately Janet was more than ready for bed. After that she played about with her letter, pretending to hide it until she thought that Anne would be thoroughly intrigued. In the end, after she had carefully set the scene, she took the letter in her hand and sidled to the door. Anne was finishing the seam on one of her nightdresses. It was pale blue with little bunches of flowers on it. Lizabet thought it was very pretty. She stopped just short of the door and said so.

"That's pretty stuff. You sew nicely."

Anne looked up with a smile.

"Do I?"

"Mmm — you do. I say, you wouldn't like to come out with me to the post, would you? Janet doesn't like my going by myself so late as this."

220

Anne ran her needle in and out of the blue stuff and put it on one side.

"Yes, I'll come, of course. It's time we went to bed anyhow."

It had been too easy. Lizabet felt all puffed up and pleased. She said in a whisper, "I don't want Janet to know. She's a fuss. And she can't say anything really — not if we're together, can she? Do you want a coat?"

"Well, perhaps. I expect it's cold outside."

"I don't want one — I'll be perfectly warm. But I'll get yours."

She was out of the door like a streak, up the stairs, and down again with Anne's coat on her arm. Janet was safe in the bathroom. How cleverly she was managing it all. And it was fun. She whispered, "Tiptoe down," and took Anne by the arm. She had it all planned out. She had been very clever about it — very clever indeed.

She opened the front door and felt the keen edge of the night's wind. It had turned much colder. As they came out on the steps, the clock of St James and St Mary in the next street began to strike eleven. Lizabet giggled and swung round.

"Oh, I'd forgotten," she said. "Don't wait for me."

"What have you forgotten?" Anne's voice was not vexed. It sounded as if she was amused.

"My other letter. Go on — I'll catch you up."

"Oh, I'll wait."

"No — no — don't. Don't wait. Go on." The last syllable died away.

Anne had the letter ready to post in her hand. She began to walk slowly in the direction of the pillar-box.

There was a car standing just short of it. As she came level with the car, a man came round it and another man got out. Before she knew that anything was going to happen it had happened. The man who had come round the car had slipped his arm about her neck. He was holding a pad of something down upon her face. She couldn't breathe. The other man caught her hands and held them in one of his. The door of the car opened and she was lifted in. She couldn't breathe. There was a ringing sound in her ears. The sound dwindled and went away.

"She's off," said the man who had come from behind the car.

CHAPTER
FORTY-TWO

Lizabet stood half-way to the corner and caught her breath to listen. There was no sound. There was no sound at all. She saw three figures together on the pavement, and then there weren't any figures. It was as sudden and as quick as that. There was no cry, no struggle. One minute there was Anne with only a little way to go to the pillar-box, and the next it had all happened. It gave her a queer excited feeling and the beginning of something that wasn't comfortable. She tossed her head, turned, and ran back to the house. She had left the door ajar. She pushed it open, took a step inside, and pushed it shut again. It was done. Anne had gone. And she wouldn't come back again.

Bewilderingly there swept over her a sense of irretrievable loss. What had she done? And quick on that something that resisted. She hadn't done anything — nothing at all. If Anne had gone with that man, she had gone of her own free will, hadn't she? She had. She had.

She went slowly up the stairs and heard Janet call from the bathroom.

"Is that you, Anne?"

"No, it's me. Anne's gone up. Do you want her?"

"No — not really — it will do in the morning."

She went on up the flight of stairs which led to her bedroom and Anne's. When she was half-way up she called down to Janet in the bathroom. "Good-night! I'm awfully sleepy." Then she ran the rest of the way and came into her room with a sense of escape.

She locked the door and sat down on the bed in the dark. She didn't want the light. And then after a few minutes she did want it and she got up and turned it on. She undressed, put the light out, and got into bed. But she couldn't sleep. Her thoughts were racing. She had been very clever, very clever indeed. There was nothing to feel uncomfortable about. What had she done?

What had she done? "I haven't done anything." Anne had lost her memory. She didn't know who she was, or where she was, or where she had come from. It was only kindness to give her back to her own people.

"*It was the basest betrayal in the world.*"

Lizabet started on her elbow. Who had said that? Someone had said it. She was in her own room, locked in. She had been comfortable and nearly asleep, and someone had said that.

It went on all night. When she was quite awake she could argue with herself. These were Anne's own people — it was much better for her to be with them. And then when she was slipping down into sleep the thought would come, "How do you know who they were, or what they wanted? How do you *know*?" Round and round, and over and over the thoughts went on.

224

There was nothing to distract your mind in the silence of the night.

The first faint breath of fear came and went. It did not stay long. It came back again. It kept on coming back until with the first faint streak of daylight it was there all the time and would not be talked down or covered up. She got out of bed, slipped on her dressing-gown, and went down to Janet's room. She couldn't bear it by herself any more. Janet would know what to do. Janet always knew.

She opened the door cautiously. Janet didn't move. She could tell by her breathing that she was asleep. A wave of self-pity came over her. Janet could sleep. She hadn't slept all night — not really. A sob came up in her throat. And at once Janet stirred and woke. She was up on her elbow looking across the faint dawn light that filled the room.

"Lizabet — what is it?"

Lizabet was child enough to dissolve into tears. She ran across to the bed and sobbed.

"Janet — oh, Janet!"

"What is it? Lizabet, what's the matter?"

"I — I couldn't sleep."

"Why couldn't you?"

"I don't know." There was a fresh and more agonized burst of tears.

Janet got out of bed.

"You're all cold," she said. "I'll get you some hot milk. Get in and cover yourself up. I won't be a minute."

It was nice and warm in Janet's bed. Perhaps she could go to sleep here. She could try. And then just as she was beginning to feel comfortably warm and sleepy Janet came back with the hot milk. Lizabet sipped the milk. Then she became aware that Janet was looking at her.

"What put you in such a state?"

Lizabet hung her head.

"I don't know."

"Something did. You'd better tell me what it was."

"It wasn't anything." Lizabet drank up the rest of the milk and pushed the glass at Janet. "It wasn't anything at all."

Janet took the glass, put it down, and turned to the bed again.

"If you don't tell me, I must go and ask Anne."

"No — no — you can't —"

"Why can't I?"

It was at that moment it came home to Lizabet that she would give almost anything for Anne to be still there. She caught Janet by the wrist and broke again into tears.

"You can't! She's not there — she's gone!"

There was a stunned silence. Then Janet said, "Where has she gone?"

"I — don't — know —"

Janet sat down on the bed. Her legs shook. She sat because she couldn't stand any longer. She said as firmly as she could, "What have you done?"

CHAPTER
FORTY-THREE

The bell rang. Miss Silver waked. She was quite composed, quite all there. She stretched out her hand to the extension by her bed, took up the receiver, and said, "Miss Silver speaking."

A voice that tried very hard to be steady answered her.

"Miss Silver, it's Janet Wells. Something dreadful has happened. Anne has gone."

"Gone!"

"Yes. I don't know what to do."

Miss Silver sat up and pulled a shawl round her.

"What has happened?"

There was a pause. It was as though Janet couldn't get it over her lips. Then she said, "I'm afraid I was followed yesterday afternoon. Lizabet went out to post a letter, and she saw the man. I'm afraid she hasn't behaved well, but she's so young — she didn't understand. She is dreadfully sorry now."

Miss Silver pressed her lips together. She said, "What did she do?"

"The man persuaded her. She thought it was a joke — I don't know what she thought. Anne was finishing some sewing and I went to have a bath. When I had gone, Lizabet pretended that she had a letter to post. She asked if Anne would come to the corner with her. She said she had promised me not to go alone when it was late. Anne went with her, and Lizabet turned back. She said she had forgotten one of her letters and would catch her up with it, so Anne walked on slowly. There was a car standing by the pillar-box. When she got level with it a man came round from the other side and another got out from the front. I — I think they held something over her face. Lizabet couldn't see, and she was frightened. She says it didn't take a minute, and then they drove away with her."

Miss Silver said, "I see —" Then she said, "Have you reported this?"

"No — not yet."

"I will tell Jim Fancourt. Do not do anything until I ring you."

She rang off, sat for a moment in thought, and then rang up Jim Fancourt.

Anne lay in the back of the car. Every now and then the deep unconsciousness which held her thinned away. She became aware of unhappy things, a confusion, of a rushing, sliding sound. As often as this happened there was the smell of chloroform again and she went down into the pits of sleep. This was until they were out of London — out of the network of roads round London.

It was later that she passed this stage. She did not hear the driver say, "I should slack it off now," or the man who was sitting by her answer with a brief "All right," but this time her consciousness came nearer and went on coming.

She made a moaning sound, and Ross Cranston said, "I say, what about it?"

The man who was driving laughed.

"She'll probably be sick. Never mind — we'll be there soon."

Ross was in a state. "Oh, I say!" he protested. The man who was driving said, "Shut up!" and he shut up.

The first thing that Anne knew was the motion of the car. At first it was pleasant and vague and then, after it had gone away and come back several times, she was tired of it and wanted it to stop. But it wouldn't stop. It went on, and on, and on. In the end she called out and tried to change her position. Something stopped her and she struggled to be free. And then the thick white giddiness came down on her again.

It was whilst she struggled out of the giddiness that they turned off from the road.

The house was in a hollow. It was thickly surrounded with trees — big hollies and monstrous yews. It was an old house. They drew up in front of it, and Anne opened her eyes again. She said, "Why have you brought me here?" Because she knew this house, she knew it very well. It was the house where she had lived with Aunt Letty, the house she had seen — was it in a dream — she didn't know. She sat in the car, her eyes wide, and every now and then the picture before her dipped and slanted. When this happened she shut her eyes and there was a rushing sound in her ears. The man who was in the car with her got out. He must have

229

gone to the door, because when she looked again it was open and he was turning and coming back to the car.

And it was Ross.

She was so astonished that she did not know what to say. For a moment she said nothing at all. She shut her eyes again, but when she opened them he was still there — her cousin Ross Cranston. She couldn't imagine what brought him there. She shut her eyes again, and then opened them quickly and said, "Ross!"

Cranston looked round. He felt the need for someone to back him up. The man who had been driving came round the house.

"That's all right," he said. "Miss Forest, will you come in? Are you able to walk?"

Anne looked at him with wavering eyes. She knew Ross — she knew this man too. He had stood in the garden at Chantreys and talked to her. He had stood in the study there and talked to Lilian. And she had stood in the dark on the other side of the door into the dining-room. She had stood there and she had listened, and then she had gone upstairs cold-foot in the dark, and dressed, and run away. She didn't know his name, but she knew who he was. He had come into the garden whilst she was there. He had talked to her. She couldn't remember all he had said, but it had frightened her. She thought he had said not to repeat anything, not to tell anyone. But she had. She had told Jim. The thought of Jim rushed to her heart. It was a strength and a deliverance. It was the linking of her two worlds. It was safety. She must keep hold of that.

230

She got out of the car. She was weak and dizzy and her head went round. She needed Ross's arm and she held on to it. They came into the hall of the house. She knew it all quite well. The third stair would creak when she put her foot on it — it always had — and the tenth one again. It was very difficult to climb the stairs, very difficult indeed. Ross was helping her. That was kind of him. He hadn't always been kind. She wouldn't think about that now.

The other man frightened her. Why had he talked to Lilian in the night, and why had she run away? She couldn't remember, but she stood still and said, "I don't want him to come up."

They weren't quite at the top — there were fifteen steps before the landing, and she had taken only twelve of them. There was a pause. She had the feeling that Ross was looking across at the other man. He had her left arm. She stood still and pulled to get it away from him, and he laughed and let it go so suddenly that she came within an ace of falling. He said, "What's the odds?" and she caught at Ross to save herself and stumbled up the rest of the stairs and across the landing. She needed Ross's arm to lean upon but not to guide her. She did not need anyone to guide her to her own room.

When she reached it, it was like coming home. The bed was sideways to the window. Someone had put a candle on the chest of drawers. She walked to the bed and laid herself down on it. She would have liked the window open, but it was too much trouble to bother about that. She pulled up the eiderdown until it covered her and turned on the pillow and went to sleep. The last thing she knew was the change from light to darkness. There was the click of a turning key. She slept.

CHAPTER
FORTY-FOUR

Jim Fancourt hung up, dressed, and went out. The first thing he did was to go round to where Anne had been. Lizabet had to face him. She didn't want to, but she had to do it. For the first time in her life she came up against the consequences of her own actions and saw them for what they were. She cried, and was told that it was no use crying — it wouldn't help her, and it wouldn't help Anne. And there was no help in Janet. She couldn't get away. She had to answer, and bit by bit the picture of what had really happened in the night came into view. And Janet stood by. She kept her there, and she made her answer. Lizabet would never have believed that she could be so cruel.

And then, before she could even burst into tears, there was Jim Fancourt asking more questions, and more, and more.

By the time they had got everything out of her and Jim had gone she was fit for nothing but to lie on her bed and cry. And Janet left her to do just that. She went out and left her all alone.

Jim Fancourt went to New Scotland Yard. He had to wait, and the time that ticked away was like endless ages. Where was she? Why had they taken her? What were they doing to her? Where was she? Interminably, over and over, the words said themselves. There was no end to them. They got him nowhere. All they did was to make it clear as daylight that if he lost Anne he lost everything in the world worth having.

He did not know how long he had to wait, but when the fresh-faced young policeman came in and said that Inspector Abbott would see him now it seemed to him as if a lifetime had gone by.

The young policeman preceded him, opened the door, announced him by name, and he came into the same room that he had been in before, with Frank Abbott looking up and giving him a friendly greeting. He said, "She's gone —" and saw Frank's face change.

"What!"

"She's gone — they've got her."

"My dear chap —"

"Everyone said don't be in a hurry, don't rush her. And what's the result? She's gone."

"Anne!"

"Yes, Anne."

"Sit down and tell me about it."

"I can't sit. I'll tell you about it — it's soon told. She's gone — that's all."

In the end he produced a fairly coherent version of Lizabet's story.

"She doesn't know what sort of car it was, and her description of the man would fit almost anyone."

Frank said tentatively, "Look here, don't be angry — It is possible that she recognized these people and went with them because she knew them."

234

"No, it's not possible! That girl admitted as much. She said the fellow put his arm round her. And there was something about a cloth on her face. She was chloroformed and carried off — I've no doubt about that. She wouldn't have gone of her own free will. I tell you she wouldn't!"

"It doesn't seem very likely. You don't think her memory came back suddenly when she saw someone she knew — someone out of her past life?"

"No, I don't. There would have been no need to chloroform her in that case. Once we got that girl Lizabet to speak, there was no doubt about it — she was chloroformed and she was carried off."

"Why?"

"I don't know. Your guess is as good as mine. Either it's money, or she knows too much — or they think she does. They must know that she saw the murdered girl. If they're not sure what she remembered, what perhaps she saw — if they don't know what she knows — don't you see she's in the most frightful danger?"

Frank nodded.

"I took up the question of who had been to see that house with the agents. We haven't been to sleep over the matter, you know. There were two orders to view — one on the twelfth, and the other on the thirteenth. The one on the thirteenth looks like the right one. It was given to a Mr Malling — an old man with a beard, very chatty. He said he wanted to take in his grandchildren for the holidays, and he thought he wanted a furnished house, but what did they think? The people at the house-agents put him down as much talk and no performance. The beard could have been a disguise. They said he kept the key overnight."

"Why did they let him go round alone? That's not usual, is it?"

"No, it isn't. I asked them the same thing, and they said he was such a nice gentleman . . . Yes, yes, I know — it's a clear case of do first and think afterwards. There are people like that, you know. What they suggest seems all right at the time. It's only afterwards that it strikes you as peculiar. And Mr Marsh who runs the place was away sick. The second string, Mr Dowding, is a nice old boy — not accustomed to taking responsibility, I should say. The house had hung on their hands. It's been left to two sisters who are *very* particular, and Mr Marsh is tired of sending people to see it. Mr Dowding was thrilled at the chance of letting it while his partner was away." Frank shrugged his shoulders.

Jim said impatiently, "Yes, I know. I saw him." He paused, and came out with, "What do we do now?"

CHAPTER
FORTY-FIVE

Anne woke up. It was early morning — very early. For a moment she did not know where she was, and then it came back to her. First of all, where she was. It was all accustomed and familiar. She was Anne Forest, and she had lived here since she was a little girl. She had lived here with Aunt Letty — Aunt Letty Forest.

She remembered.

She remembered Aunt Letty bringing her to the house for the first time. It was a very dim memory that came and went. There was a big black dog. She could see his curled shining coat, but she couldn't remember his name. They played together on a grass lawn behind the house, and Aunt Letty came and called her in to tea. She remembered the currant buns, how good they tasted. After that there was a long stretch when she didn't remember anything at all, or only little bits. Aunt Letty was there all the time. Sometimes there were battles between them. One she remembered very distinctly. It was a hot, bright day in summer. It was hot and bright, but there must have been rain, because all along one side of the road there were little pools and puddles. And as she walked Anne trod in the puddles and splashed. It was lovely, but Aunt Letty didn't think so. Aunt Letty said, "Stop at once, you naughty child!" How funny to remember a thing like that after all these years. Aunt Letty was gone — three years ago. It was three years since Anne had stood at the door and waited for the cab to come and take her away — three years since Aunt Letty's funeral — three years since she was twenty-one. Dear Aunt Letty — dear, *dear* Aunt Letty. The loss of her came as fresh as if she had died yesterday instead of three years ago.

The tears came fresh to her eyelids as she thought of that last day. She had gone out, and when she was half-way to the village she found that she had left her purse and she turned back. Then, when she was close among the bushes in the front of the house, she had heard the sound. She had heard it, but she didn't know what it was. There was a crash and a fall. She had to describe them over and over again, and she couldn't get nearer than that. But when she came round the house, there was Aunt Letty fallen down by the back door with a terrible wound in her head. She wasn't quite dead, but she died before the doctor came, and she died without recovering consciousness.

Anne lay there and remembered. There was no clue — nothing at all. Someone had killed Aunt Letty. Someone had struck her a smashing blow and made off through the woods. There was nothing to say who it was.

The house was left to Anne. Nobody wanted to take it, because of the murder. Everyone said that Anne couldn't stay there. She didn't want to stay there. She wanted to go away as far as possible and never see the place again. At least she thought that that was what she wanted. She went away.

She went right away, round the world with her friend Mavis Enderby. It was curious that all the time of being away seemed so dim. They had gone round the world and turned to come home through America. Try as she would, she couldn't remember all that as she remembered the little bits and pieces of her childhood. And then Mavis had fallen in love with a chance-met stranger and had married him — just like that. And Anne had said she couldn't think how anyone could do such a thing, but it was all right for Mavis if she wanted to. She didn't know how she could, but it was her life, and she had nothing against Bill, who was nice but no different from hundreds of other men whom they had met.

What makes you fall in love with one and not with another? What had made her fall in love with Jim and he with her? They had both met dozens of other people. There was everything to stop them, and yet they had both gone down drowning deep.

She sat up and looked around the room. It was her own room. In the early morning light it had a shabby, familiar look. She got out of bed and went to the window. The trees had grown. They had not been cut or pruned, and they crowded upon one another. Her room looked to the back of the house. There used to be a gap between the two end cherry trees, and you could see right down the hill to Swan Eaton. Now there was no gap. The trees closed it in. You couldn't see the village, or any habitation.

For the first time since she had wakened Anne began to feel afraid. She didn't know what she was afraid of, but fear came silting over her and she drew back from the window as if the fear were outside in the garden among the trees.

But that was nonsense. Nonsense or not, she went right back from the window until she touched the bed and sat down on it, shaking a little. She was remembering — that was why she was afraid. She had landed from the States and gone to London. She hadn't written to say she was coming. That is to say, she hadn't given any exact date. She had been away for nearly three years, and she had waited to see Mavis married, and then she had come. There wasn't anyone very near — some cousins whom she had never seen much of. She remembered arriving in London on a dark rainy evening. She remembered going to an hotel. And she couldn't remember anything more than that. It seemed very far away and vague, but she did remember getting to the hotel in the evening and being very tired. And after that nothing — nothing at all until she was standing half-way down those cellar steps and knowing that there was a girl's dead body at their foot. She didn't strain to remember. Perhaps it would come back. It was no good straining. There was a gap in her mind. She couldn't fill it up by trying, but at least she knew who she was now.

There was a clock on the mantelpiece. She looked up for it as if she expected it to be there. Someone must have wound it. It said half-past six. She tried the door and found it locked. Her clothes were here, and there was water in the jug on the washstand. She washed, dressed, and felt more ready to face things.

There were the two men here — her cousin Ross Cranston and the other man whose name she didn't know. She wasn't really afraid of Ross. He had come and gone, always rather unsatisfactory and a trouble to Aunt Letty, but she had never thought of him as someone to be afraid of. It was the other man who made her feel as if a cold finger touched her spine. She didn't know his name. She only knew that he was evil, and that she stood in his way. What happens to you when you stand in the way of an evil person?

She made herself look at the answer to that.

CHAPTER
FORTY-SIX

Anne went on remembering. It was here a little and there a little. Then, suddenly, something that made sense of a lot of things. She sat in her bedroom, and in her mind she went round the house. Every time she did this she remembered something fresh. You couldn't push your memories, they just came. And they came in the funniest way. It was when she was going up the attic stair in her mind that she remembered why she had gone to the London hotel, and it's name, the Hood.

Aunt Letty had always stayed there. It was the sort of hotel where ladies like Aunt Letty stay — very dignified, rather expensive, thoroughly respectable. It had not the faintest connection with the attics, and why she should remember it when she was thinking about going up the attic stair in this house she couldn't imagine.

She put the hotel away and went on picking her way round the house. She had been going up the attic stair — she would go on. The stair was very steep. She could remember Aunt Letty telling her to be careful as she came and went. She even remembered what she had said ... No, that wasn't Aunt Letty — that was Grammy. How curious to have no consciousness at all of someone, and then to have her back as if she had never been away. Dear, dear Grammy, who was the cook until the second year of the war, when she left to take charge of her sister's children when her sister had been killed by a bomb. Grammy had always said, "Now you mind your feet, my dear. Don't you look at them and don't you hurry them, and you won't fall."

The attic was large and dark. Anne always thought it was like a hospital, because there were broken things everywhere — a screen with a hole in the panel, a chair with a broken leg, a picture with a broken frame. She remembered so many broken things. How strange that she could remember these things which had never mattered very much — remember them quite accurately and distinctly as she sat on the side of her bed in a locked room on the floor below — things that she hadn't seen or thought of for three years. And yet she couldn't remember what had happened so short a time ago.

The attic — it was curious how she came back to it. Perhaps it was an association of ideas. She would have to think that out. Everything in the attic was mixed up, nothing was in order. That was how her mind was — old things, new things. Not so many of those. Things that had had their value and lost it, things that had never had any value at all. In her mind's eye she stood in the doorway of the attic and looked into its dimly lighted depths. There seemed to be no end to the things that were in it, as there was no end to the things that were in her mind — things half forgotten, things half remembered, things that showed vaguely and were half glimpsed and then wholly lost again. Time went by.

The house began to stir. Someone came along the passage. The key turned in the lock. Anne sat quite still. The handle turned, and the door opened a very little way. Ross's voice said her name.

"Anne —"

She said, "Yes."

"How are you? Do you feel like getting up?"

She said, "Yes," again.

"Are you all right?"

"Yes."

He stayed for a minute, twisting the handle, not opening the door any more, and then shutting it carefully so as not to make any noise. He went downstairs then, moving very quietly and carefully.

Anne found herself laughing. That was Ross all over, to get himself into an indefensible position and not have the courage to brazen it out. She remembered that she had always despised him, and that cheered her. He had not locked the door when he had gone, so she was no longer a prisoner. She went to the bathroom, emptied the water she had washed in, made her bed. She began to wonder whether she was alone with Ross — whether the other man was gone. She did not count on it, but she wondered.

When she had finished the things she had to do she went to the dressing-table and looked at herself in the glass. There were dark marks under her eyes that did not please her. She thought she looked as if she had been ill. She rubbed her cheeks, and then wished that

244

she hadn't. It was all right for her to look pale. Besides, it didn't matter how she looked.

She went downstairs. Someone was frying bacon and sausages. She came into the kitchen and saw the other man. As always, the sight of him did things to her courage. She felt the same horrid inward shaking that had come on her in the garden at Chantreys when she had looked up and seen him leaning against the gate. But this time she was at some pains to hide her fear. She was horribly afraid, but she mustn't let him see it.

"Ah, you've waked," he said.

"Yes."

"Ross said you'd be down. We brought the bacon with us. No sense in making talk in the village."

"I suppose not."

He burst out laughing.

"Very cool and calm, aren't you! Going to be a sensible girl?"

Anne made herself look at him. She kept her eyes level and calm on his.

"It depends on what you mean by sensible."

He gave her an insolent look.

"Do what you're told. Make yourself useful. Speak when you're spoken to. Hold your tongue when you're bid."

"Why should I?"

He set down his pan of sausages a little to one side of the fire and came towards her. Anne went back as far as she could go. The wall stopped her, and she stood. He put his hands on her shoulders and looked down on her.

"You'll do as you're told," he said. "Is that quite clear? Is it? *Is it?*" His voice didn't get any louder, it softened. That softening of a harsh voice was the most horrible thing that Anne had ever heard.

A dizziness came over her. She tried to keep her head up and her eyes steady. His eyes were like a hawk's, dominant, ferocious. She couldn't go any farther back. And then there was a footstep outside, and she called out. He said on a low growling note, "You watch your step," and turned round and went back to the fire.

When Ross came in she was so glad to see him that it was all she could do not to show it. It was all she could do, but she did it. To let them know how terribly afraid she was would be to give away her last scrap of protection. She moved to a chair and sat down.

It was at this moment that she remembered everything.

CHAPTER
FORTY-SEVEN

"He said he'd let us know."

"Then he will do so," said Miss Silver firmly.

Jim stood looking out into the street, his back to the room.

"And if he has nothing to tell?"

Miss Silver was knitting. She looked compassionately across the football sweater destined for her niece Ethel Burkett's eldest boy and said, "He will have something. I am sure of it."

"And if he has not?"

Miss Silver did not reply. The most trying moments in human experience were those in which there was nothing to be done except to wait. They were especially trying for a man whose previous training had been one of action. Her mind sought for something which would relieve this tension and give him something to do.

She said, "You were going to show me Anne's bag."

He half turned with an impatient jerk of the shoulders.

"There's nothing there."

"Nevertheless I should like to see it. You did bring it away, did you not?"

"Oh, yes, I brought it away. There's nothing in it — except the money."

"I should like to see it."

"I tell you there's nothing in it."

Miss Silver knitted in silence. At a less hazardous moment she would have implied some reproof, but this was not the time for reproof, and what had begun by being a mere distraction to relieve a most trying time of waiting had now assumed an importance which she could neither justify nor abandon. When she was quite sure that she could speak in her usual controlled manner she said, "Mr Fancourt, I do not wish to be troublesome, but I would greatly appreciate it if you would show me that bag."

He turned from the window to face her.

"There's nothing in it."

"Will you let me see that for myself? I do not wish to be tiresome, or to give you extra to do, but I would appreciate it —"

All at once he was as anxious to go as he had been obstinately fixed to stay. Anything was better than to count the moments whilst they prolonged themselves into endless time.

Miss Silver continued to knit. It would take him an hour to go to his rooms and get the bag — at least an hour. It would be much better for him than counting the moments and eating his heart out.

It was just over the hour when Emma Meadows let him in. He certainly looked better, and Miss Silver congratulated herself. Even if there were no other result, the expedition would have been well worth while. He was holding the bag loose and unwrapped. Emma Meadows had barely shut the door upon him before he said, "There's nothing there — nothing at all. I knew there wasn't."

Miss Silver put down the almost finished sweater and held out her hand.

"May I see?"

He repeated, "There's nothing," handed the bag over, and flung himself down in the chair with its back to the window.

Miss Silver took the bag and opened it. She told herself that she expected nothing, but as her hands touched the clasp she knew that she was going to find something. She couldn't say how she knew it, but she did know it. Yet when she opened the bag it seemed to be quite empty. Jim had taken out the notes and the little change that was left in the purse and put them away. The bag was empty — a black bag with a grey lining, and in the middle an inner compartment divided down the centre, one half grey, and one white kid for a powderpuff. The little purse at the side was quite empty. It had held coppers and silver. Miss Silver remembered that she had seen Anne looking amongst notes and change for something that would tell her who she was, where she came from, and where she was going. There had been a letter between the side purse and the one in the middle. Now there wasn't anything there at all.

Miss Silver felt an acute disappointment as she let the bag fall into her lap. And then in that very moment she knew that her premonition had been real, for as the bag dropped she was aware of something faint but quite unmistakable.

Jim said impatiently, "There's nothing there. I've looked."

But Miss Silver picked up the bag again. "I am not so sure," she said.

She began to turn the bag inside out. There was a little dust and a shred or two of paper. And then, down at the bottom where the side seam ended, there was a little hole. It wasn't hole in the stuff. It was just a careless bit of work in a new bag, a fold pressed over and not stitched down. You could have looked in the bag a hundred times and not have seen it, but it was just the place where a little twist of paper might stick and hide itself.

There was a little twist of paper there. Jim got up from his chair and watched while Miss Silver fished for it with one of her knitting-needles and finally brought it out. It was quite a small piece. It had on it two addresses, one stamped and the other written. The stamped address said "*The Hood Hotel*", *Mayville Street*, and a telephone number. The written name was in Anne's handwriting — *Miss Anne Forest, Yew Tree Cottage, Swan Eaton, Sussex.*

Jim said, "How on earth —" and then stopped.

Miss Silver went on looking at the address. Anne Forest, Yew Tree Cottage, Swan Eaton — That was her name and her address, then. But how did it come to be here in the other girl's bag? This *was* the other girl's bag — the dead girl's bag — the girl who had been murdered in the empty house. What had Anne's name and Anne's address to do with her?

She lifted her eyes very gravely to Jim's face and said, "I think we must ring up the hotel."

Jim said in a stumbling voice, "What does it mean?"

Miss Silver said, "It means we have Anne's name and, I think, her address."

"You think that is her name?"

"I should say so. It looks to me as if the murdered girl was staying in the same hotel, and as if Anne Forest had given her this address."

"I don't see how that could have been."

"We cannot expect to see plainly all at once. We shall know more when we have rung up the hotel." She crossed over to the writing-table, took up the telephone, and gave the number of the Hood Hotel.

Jim came to stand beside her. He could not hear what was said at the desk of the hotel. There was a running murmur of sound, and every now and then Miss Silver's voice intervening to ask a question. The questions were what he could have asked himself. It was maddening not to be able to distinguish the answers.

"You had a Miss Anne Forest staying with you about a fortnight ago?" That was the first question.

Miss Silver gave him a nod. Yes, they had had a Miss Anne Forest staying there. They still had her luggage. She had gone out and had not returned. They were much concerned, but she had been talking of going to visit friends, and they hadn't liked to take any action. All the same —

Miss Silver continued, "Did you also have a Mrs Fancourt staying in the hotel?"

No, there had been no Mrs Fancourt.

It was a blow. If she had not been staying at the same hotel, how had the two girls met? There was just one more chance. Miss Silver took it. She had not a great deal of hope, but she would ask the question. She asked it. "Did you perhaps have a Miss Anne Borrowdale staying with you?"

More to her surprise than she would have been ready to admit, the voice at the other end of the line immediately replied in quite an animated manner.

"Oh, yes, she was here. And she left on the same day as Miss Forest did. That was one reason why we did not think very seriously about Miss Forest leaving us. She had made friends with Miss Borrowdale, and we took it for granted that they had gone away together. I hope there is nothing wrong?"

Miss Silver replied in a grave voice.

"I hope not. I am ringing up for Mr Fancourt."

She put a few more questions, then replaced the receiver and turned round.

"They were both staying at the Hood."

"How? Why?"

"I do not know. There are several ways that it could have happened. Anne, the one who is dead, was here. Anne, the one who is alive, had landed from America. She had just landed. That would account for her not being missed here. The girl at the hotel said she had been round the world with a friend who had married and had stayed in America. They would have been

252

more concerned if she had not left all her boxes — there were a good many of them. And then the maid who had waited on her had met with an accident and been taken to hospital. They thought it possible that Anne Forest had told her something that would account for her absence. It could happen quite easily. As regards the other Anne, the girl who was killed, she had very little luggage."

"I can't think how she came to be in the hotel at all. I sent her to the Birdstocks to wait until she heard from Lilian."

Miss Silver was silent for a moment. Then she said, "If she was the girl who visited Mrs Birdstock and received your aunt's letter — and I think she must have been — she was a free agent then. Had she a foreign accent?"

Jim considered.

"No — not noticeably."

There were a few minutes' silence. Then Miss Silver took up the telephone again.

"I think we should let Inspector Abbott know," she said.

CHAPTER
FORTY-EIGHT

Anne felt her head go round and clear. She knew everything now. She had remembered everything. She was thankful for the chair which had been handy. She might have fallen. She had not fallen. The chair held her up. Her head would settle in a moment. Ross didn't look at her or speak to her. He was ashamed. And the other man had gone to the fire, and stood with his back to her and prodded sausages with a fork.

She remembered everything with astonishing clarity. Coming to the hotel. The chambermaid who came to her room — a pale girl, rather pretty. She remembered what she had for dinner, and that she had been tired and had gone up early to bed, but she had not slept well. It had been a curious night. She couldn't remember one just like it — rushing images, dreams that came and went, and went and came again. And then the morning — the girl. It was all quite clear in her mind. She came into the dining-room for breakfast and looked for a table, and there over by the window there was a table for two, and there was a girl sitting at it. There was something in her face like a lost kitten. Anne found herself walking towards her. She pulled out the other chair and said, "Do you mind if I sit here?"

and the girl's face had lighted up. "Yes, do," she said. "Oh, do!"

It was extraordinary how clear it all was. The girl who was dead in the cellar was alive again. Her voice rang in Anne's ears — a pretty voice with something that was not quite an accent. She got up from her chair and crossed to the door. She couldn't sit here and remember — she couldn't.

Just as she reached the door Ross turned round. He said, "Where are you off to? Breakfast will be ready in five minutes."

Anne answered him steadily. "I won't be long. Don't wait." She heard the other man laugh as she went out of the door and up the stairs.

In her room she sat down on her bed and went on remembering. That poor child — her ignorance, her folly, and the last glimpse she had of her lying dead at the foot of the steps in a strange house. She had poured the whole thing out. "My name is Anne Borrowdale. Well, I don't know whether it is or not. Perhaps it's Anne Fancourt. That sounds funny, doesn't it?" And she had laughed as if it was all a joke. And then more of that tumbling speech with the something that was not quite an accent running through it. "You see, I don't know whether I'm really married or not. My father, he was killed." Her voice went suddenly into tears and she put out her two hands to clasp Anne's strange ones that didn't seem strange any longer. "They were blasting, and a great stone hit him. Jim said he had run forward. I don't know how it happened, but it did happen. The stone crushed him, and when he knew that he would die he wanted Jim to marry me, and the priest came and we were married. And he died." Her tone lightened. It flung away the past. "And the aeroplane came down." She clapped her hands together. "An American plane that was off its course and must come down. We watched it come nearer and nearer. You don't know how exciting it was! And when it was down there were two young men in it, and Jim asked them would they take me with them. At first they said no, and then they said yes. That was after Jim talked to them. He told them he had married me, and that it was a matter of life and death to get me out of the country — a matter of life or death. The Russians are very particular about their nationals not going to other countries, and a Russian woman's child is a Russian, no matter what the father may be. They would not let me go, and Jim had promised my father." The two hands were clapped together and she concluded, "So you see he persuaded those Americans to bring me with them. And they did."

Anne remembered her own puzzled frown. She could hear the tone of voice in which she said, "And what are you doing here?" The girl laughed. It came back to Anne how easily she had laughed, and come near to weeping. Now it was the turn of laughter. "Well, I thought" — her face screwed up in the funniest way like a little cat — "I thought all my life I will have to do what Jim says. He is my husband. But I have money here — a lot of money from my father. Why should I not spend a little? Why must I go to that parlourmaid's house? And I think I will not go. I will go to the hotel my father always talked about, and I will amuse myself.

I am a married lady — it is all quite proper. So I post Jim's letter to his Aunt Lilian who lives at Chantreys, Haleycott. And then I think what I will do to amuse myself."

That was how it had gone — gay, inconsequent chatter — in the middle of it all something struggling up in her own mind, until quite suddenly she came out with "What did you say your father's name was?"

The girl stopped.

"My father?" Tragedy swept across her mood. "Oh, my poor father — such a terrible way to die! What did you want to know?"

"His name."

"I told you — Borrowdale."

"His Christian names?" She could see the girl's sudden suspicious state.

She said, "Why?"

And her own answer, "Because I think — I think we may be related."

"Oh —"

"I shall know if you tell me his names."

"Leonard Maurice Forest Borrowdale."

Anne said, "I am Anne Forest. I think we are cousins."

It hurt still — the girl's pleasure, her excitement. She was like flashing water — there were tears — smiles. It all hurt too much to remember.

From down below came the sound of a man's footsteps.

"What are you doing? Aren't you coming down to breakfast?"

It went through her mind that they didn't trust her. When you had done murder you couldn't trust anyone. That was one of the ways in which evil punished itself. She called back, "I will come when I have finished what I am doing." She was remembering. When she had finished remembering she would go down. She couldn't remember under the eyes of those two men. Were they both murderers? She didn't know.

Ross called back and said, "Your bacon will be cold." Then he went into the dining-room. But he didn't shut the door when he went in. He left it open so that he would hear when she came down the stairs. They didn't trust her. There was no reason why they should trust her. There was murder between them. She went on thinking. The girl had stopped her excited chatter. A look of guilt came over her face. She put a hand to her lips, looked at Anne, and said, "Oh —"

"What is it?"

"I forgot."

"What did you forget?"

"I wasn't to tell anyone — I wasn't to speak of anything. What shall I do?"

Anne remembered that she had laughed, and she had said quite lightly, "Well, it's too late now. And if we're cousins it doesn't matter."

How had they known she would be a danger to them? It wasn't a thing you could guess. How did they *know?* The poor child would have talked to anyone. She was utterly innocent, utterly unprotected. But how did they know that she needed protection?

258

And then there was the child telling her — "I am married, you know, but here I thought I would be Miss Borrowdale." She went into a little rippling laugh. "So I wrote all my names in the register — I wrote Anne Forest Borrowdale. It looked nice!" And she laughed again.

It was heartbreaking to remember, but she had to go on. Anne Forest Borrowdale — she saw it all in one horrid searing flash. Ross Forest Cranston — her cousin — this poor girl's cousin. Her own name — Anne Forest. The three names wove together in her mind. For a moment she lost herself in the giddy whirl of realization. Then it all cleared to a deadly cold certainty. She sat in that cold certainty and looked at the facts that faced her there.

She was coming home after three years' absence. She had written to say she was coming. She had written to the hotel and to her cousins the Cranstons — to Ross's cousins. So he had known. She didn't know where the other man came in — the man Maxton. He would be someone Ross knew. He was evil through and through. And Ross? She didn't know. He had always been difficult. Aunt Letty had troubled about him a lot — Aunt Letty who would have been heartbroken if she had lived. Aunt Letty hadn't lived. For the first time the dreadful idea came to her that Ross might know why Aunt Letty had died — and how. And she knew when the thought came that it had been there for a long, long time. She wouldn't look at it, she wouldn't think of it. She had put it away, but now it came out of the shadows in her mind and stood there plain to see. She made herself look at it, and then turned back.

She was herself, asking the little cousin how she had come to the Hood, and she had the answer bubbling up between tears and laughter. "Oh, my father — he always spoke of the Hood. We made such wonderful plans, he and I. How we would come to London and stay at the Hood, and go to the theatre, and see *everything*!"

She had it all. The only part she didn't know was the end. She didn't know how they had persuaded her little cousin to steal a march on her and go round to the house where she had been found dead. She didn't know why her death had been decided on. She could guess that it had been precipitated by her own arrival. Only why — why — *why*?

She went over what she had done herself on that morning. She had been out all day — to the bank, shopping. And then she remembered that she had been very tired, so tired that she had . . . What had she done? Try as she would, she couldn't remember.

And then quite suddenly it was there, just when she turned away and thought, "I won't go on. It doesn't matter." She saw herself walking down the passage, putting in the key, and opening the door. And there was the note on her dressing-table: "I'm going round to see someone. I'm going with — I won't say who. I'll tell you in the evening. It's all very exciting. I'm going to number 109 Greyville Road. Anne." She saw herself reading it through — reading it three times. The note must have been given to that nice girl the chamber-maid. She saw herself standing, turning the note round, and then seeing the little squiggle of writing in the corner: "Perhaps I'll tell you now. One of them is a man called Maxton. I don't like him very much. The other is our cousin Ross Cranston. I'm meeting them there."

She had met them, and she had met her death. She saw herself in front of the dressing-table, reading the words.

What had she done with the letter? She remembered putting it somewhere. Where? It wasn't on her after her visit to Greyville Road. But she had dropped her bag there. That was how they had known that she had followed Anne. That was how Maxton had come on her track to Haleycott. It wasn't in the bag that she had dropped, she felt quite sure about that. And then she remembered that she had put the letter into her handkerchief-case. She didn't know why she had done that, but she had. She could see herself standing there with the drawer open, putting the letter away. She didn't know why she had put it away so carefully, she only knew that she had. And then, tired as she was, she had gone downstairs again and walked to the corner and taken a taxi. She even remembered that she had asked the driver whether he knew Greyville Road, and when he said he did she asked to be put down at the corner. Why had she done that? It seemed quite a rational thing to do at the time. She remembered that. Well, then she ought to be able to remember why it had seemed so sensible. She thought it was because she didn't want to be too obviously following her little cousin. Yes, that was it. She had paid off her taxi at the corner and walked along to number 109, and she had gone up the steps and found the door unlatched. Why was it unlatched? And the answer to that came too. It was because her cousin Anne lay dead in the cellar. It was the last, cruellest trick. It was the trap to involve whoever came next to this door, honest man or thief.

And she herself had walked into the trap.

CHAPTER
FORTY-NINE

Anne got to her feet. She must go down. It was the most difficult thing she had ever done in her life. It had got to be done. She must go down and eat her breakfast, and she mustn't show that she had remembered. She wondered at their bringing her here, but they had got to take her somewhere, and they didn't know that it would mean anything to her. They didn't know that her memory would come back. She mustn't let them know about that. She mustn't stay up here any longer, or they would get suspicious. She must watch every word, every look. She must watch her very thoughts. She felt a sudden rush of courage and of hope. Without giving herself time to think or be afraid she went down the stairs and into the dining-room.

Ross was watching the door. He said, "You've been a long time," and he said it in a complaining sort of voice.

She said, "I felt queer. I'm all right now. I think I want my breakfast."

Maxton was eating hot buttered toast. He waved it at her and said, "We're not starving you. Come along and have breakfast."

It was a curious meal. There was no attempt to make her take anything apart from the general stock. She could cut from the loaf and she could boil herself an egg. She could drink tea out of the teapot and milk from the milk-jug. She made a good meal, and felt better for it. What next?

What was their plan? They must have one. She had eaten in silence, but when she had finished she pushed back her chair and got up.

"Why have you brought me here?" she said.

Maxton swung round to look at her. He did not get up. She would not look at him. She looked instead at Ross Cranston — her cousin Ross Forest Cranston. That was one thing that she had — she knew that Ross was her cousin, she knew that his middle name was Forest, and he didn't know that she knew these things. She must keep her head. They mustn't know that she had got her memory back. It was dangerous enough for them to know who she was, but once they knew that she had got her memory back it would be the end — for her.

All these thoughts were in her mind together. They were quite distinct and clear. They took no time at all. They were there.

It was Maxton who spoke. She did not look at him, but she knew that he was smiling as he said, "Brought you here? Now I wonder why we did."

She put up a hand and passed it across her eyes.

"Why did you?" she said, and her voice trembled in spite of herself. It wasn't deliberate, but she thought afterwards that she couldn't have done better. The thought slid into her mind and out again.

Maxton laughed.

264

"We thought it would be a nice quiet place for you to make up your mind in. It's the fortunate girl you are, you know, to have two men to choose from and perfect peace and quiet to do it in."

She spoke quickly, unguardedly.

"What do you mean?"

She was looking at him now. Her eyes hated what they saw. He smiled, and it was all she could do not to throw anything she could reach at him. If she were to give way to that, it would be the end, and she knew it. Their eyes met, clashed. She looked away. She looked at Ross. He sat sullen, not looking at her, and drew on the tablecloth with his fork. She spoke to him.

"What does he mean?"

But it was Maxton who answered her.

"I mean that you're a lucky girl. You've got a choice. You can take the one of us you like best, and after a month's honeymoon, or maybe longer if you're obstinate, we'll get a special licence, and we'll make it all quite legal and moral for you in your aunt's own parish church. Whichever of us you choose, he'll be man enough to see you don't change your mind. Now which is it to be — your cousin Ross or myself? You can have the day to make up your mind. And it's no good thinking you can run away, because we'll both be here waiting anxiously for your decision."

She went back a step, her two hands at her breast, her eyes on Ross. He was jabbing the fork into the cloth. She said faintly, "What does he mean?"

Ross turned away from her, turned to Maxton and said, "I told you she doesn't know."

Anne held on to herself. Of the two she was much, much less afraid of Ross. It might be possible — she didn't know . . . She said in a wondering, frightened tone, "Are you my cousin?" and he said, "Yes." She turned to face him. "What does he mean?"

Ross didn't answer. He was looking at Maxton. She moved back a step. Maxton nodded carelessly.

"Go along and think it over," he said. "You can have your cousin Ross, or you can have me. That's more choice than many would give you, and more choice than many would get. You can have him, or you can have me, and you can have a day to think it over — not any longer. If you don't choose, we'll toss for you and let the best man win."

She went backwards step by step as he spoke. He filled her with such fear and disgust that she could not be sure that she would not faint. She looked at Ross and saw that there was no help in him. There was no help in anyone except herself. She reached the door and put out her hand behind her to open it. She went out without turning, and so to the stairs. Then she turned with a slow and stiff motion and went up to her room and locked herself in.

CHAPTER
FIFTY

"It's about forty miles," said Frank Abbott. "There's no particular reason why they should be there, you know."

"There's no particular reason why they should be anywhere," said Jim. He stood looking out of the window in Frank Abbott's room, plainly beyond all thought or reason, actuated solely by a frantic desire for action.

Frank turned to Miss Silver. She sat very upright at the far side of his table. She wore the black coat which had endured for many years and would not be discarded whilst it endured. Her neat, pale features were perfectly composed, the lips firmly set, the eyes attentive. The hands in their black gloves were crossed firmly on the handle of a worn black handbag. Her second-best hat of black felt, adorned by a large bow of black and purple ribbon, was tilted a little more over her face than she usually wore it. To Frank Abbott her appearance and demeanour were the clearest indications that she had made up her mind. He might go, or he might stay, but Miss Silver was going down to Swan Eaton. All that depended upon him was whether she went alone, or whether she went accompanied and protected by the forces of the law. He said, "I suppose you have made up your mind?"

Miss Silver replied in a most decorous manner.

"I believe that it would be a good plan to go down to Swan Eaton."

"And suppose they are not there?"

"That we can consider if the occasion offers."

"You really think —"

"I think that there are indications in that direction. I think that we must explore them. And I think that there is no time to be lost."

Jim swung round on them.

"Do you realize what may be happening whilst we are talking? Either you go at once, or I go alone! They may be murdering her!"

Miss Silver rose to her feet.

"It would be better if you would come with us, Frank," she said, "but Mr Fancourt and I are leaving immediately."

Frank Abbott nodded.

"All right, you win. Give me a quarter of an hour, and I'll collect Hubbard and a car."

It was a little more than a quarter of an hour before they started. The clock on Frank's mantelpiece stood, in fact, at eleven-thirty before they left the room. Jim endured. Every moment was an hour of torment. Whilst they fleeted away the time — time went on. It passed — it would not come again. What was happening happened. The dead would not come back to life. They were gone. Jim stood at the window and stared out with eyes that saw nothing. "Anne — Anne

— Anne — *Anne!*" He half cried out her name. He heard nothing else, was aware of nothing else. Time went by.

The first thing he knew was Miss Silver's hand on his arm and her voice saying, "We are quite ready now, Mr Fancourt."

It was a relief to be in motion. Frank Abbott sat in the front of the car with young Hubbard. Jim and Miss Silver were at the back. She did not speak, but sat there with her hands crossed upon her bag and her face pale and still. Jim did not notice her at all. He sat upright, his hands clenched. However fast the car went, he was pushing it a little faster. When Hubbard slowed down to the traffic, he was pushing with all his strength to get him on again. And all the time his mind ran ahead and called on Anne.

Anne lay on her bed in the room where she had slept as a child. She had prayed, and she had come into peace. She didn't even know what was going to happen, but she wouldn't believe that evil would have the victory — she couldn't believe that. She didn't know how she would be saved. She only knew that something would save her. She lay on her bed and watched the changing light and the shadows of the trees outside. Presently she slept.

Down in the village the car stopped to ask the way.

"Yew Tree Cottage?" That was Frank Abbott.

The first person he asked did not seem to know. He began, "I'm a stranger here —" but Frank did not wait for anything more.

He tried again, and this time got an answer.

269

"Yew Tree Cottage? Oh, yes. But there won't be no one there. Empty, that's what it's been these three years ever since Miss Forest was murdered."

Jim's hands tightened. The nails dug into the palms of his hands. She wasn't here — she wasn't anywhere. Where was she? Anne — Anne — *Anne!*

The man, who was chewing a straw, went on chewing it.

"Oh, yes, I can tell you how to get there. But no one's lived in the house since Miss Forest was murdered. It belongs to her niece, and she's abroad . . . Oh, she's back, is she? Well, she hasn't been down here." He was interminably slow, but in the end they got the direction.

What was the use? She wasn't here, she wasn't anywhere. He had missed his chance. Her name came and went in his mind like a voice calling.

Someone else was calling that name. Anne woke up. For a moment she did not know where she was. She had been in a dream. It had been pleasant in her dream. She walked in a cool wood. There was heat abroad and she was aware of the sounds of traffic, but she was in a quiet place. She heard the sound of wheels, but where she was there was peace and silence.

With the first of her returning sense the sound was clearer. The shadow of the trees wavered and was gone. She opened her eyes and saw a room, windows, the dark branch of a yew tree, and the clock on the mantelpiece. The clock said a quarter past one. The sound of wheels which had waked her had stopped. Her heart quickened. She was here, in Aunt Letty's cottage, in great danger. That was the first thought. And then there was a second. Had she really heard a car, and if so, what car?

She jumped up and went to the window. The car had stopped. There was a murmur of voices. What voices? Whose?

Downstairs the two men sat frozen. They had heard a car draw up. The car in which they had come was in the garage, with the door shut. Was it shut? Maxton had been in, and had come out, and had shut the door. He was sure about that. What he wasn't sure about was whether Ross had been in since. He fixed his eyes upon him, and Ross shook his head. He'd do that anyhow. Neither of them spoke. It wasn't any good. The kitchen fire was on. The coal was damp. It was smoking. No one would believe the place was empty.

Maxton got up and went to the door. He opened it a little way and said, "What is it?"

Three men and an elderly woman. Three men, and one of them Fancourt. He said roughly, "What is it?"

Frank Abbott was out of the car. The other two men were getting out. Maxton kept hold of the door and nearly closed it. Anger burst in him, leaving no room for fear.

Jim Fancourt said, "Where's Anne?" and Maxton raised his eyebrows.

"Why ask me?" he said.

Jim Fancourt repeated what he had said before.

"Where is Anne?"

Maxton heard the door of the room upstairs open — the door of Anne's room. He banged the front door in

Jim's face and sprang backwards. Anne came out on the landing and stood at the top of the stairs looking down. He called "Ross!" but there wasn't any answer.

Frank Abbott left the car standing and ran round the house. He got in at the back door, to see Maxton charging up the stairs with a pistol in his hand, and Anne standing on the top step looking down. As his feet sounded in the hall, Maxton looked back, his face mad with anger, his pistol in his hand. He fired. The noise of the shot seemed to fill the hall.

Jim Fancourt left battering at the front door and broke the drawing-room window. Inside, Anne ran quickly down the three or four steps which separated her from Maxton and pushed at him with all her might. If he had been still facing her she might have pushed in vain, but he was turned from her, his feet on two levels as he had turned at the sound of Frank Abbott's rush, and the unexpected thrust pushed him off his balance. He lost it, clutched at her, missed, and fell sprawling. The pistol flew from his hand, knocked on the balustrade, and fell into the hall. By the time Jim emerged from the drawing-room he lay in a heap at the foot of the stairs with Frank Abbott and Hubbard bending over him.

Miss Silver, descending from the car without haste, was aware of the noise. She heard the fall — the shot, and she had reached the broken window, when she became aware of Ross Cranston edging round the house. She did not know him, but he had a guilty look. She turned and spoke.

"What are you doing here?"

272

He swore, and ran away. Into the wood, tearing his clothes on the brambles, thinking of nothing but how he might get away.

Miss Silver watched him out of sight and turned back to the house. From what she could hear, the fight was over. Listening at the broken window, she discerned Jim's voice speaking to Anne. It was a voice broken with emotion no doubt perfectly satisfactory to its recipient. Frank Abbott's voice was also audible. It was addressing remarks of a hostile nature to Mr Maxton.

Miss Silver considered it highly unnecessary that she should either remain outside or take the risk of cutting herself upon the broken glass of the window. She advanced to the door and rapped upon it with the knocker.

CHAPTER
FIFTY-ONE

It did not take long to find Ross Cranston. He had fallen and sprained an ankle in the wood and there was no fight in him. They put him handcuffed into the car with Frank Abbott between him and Maxton and drove to the nearest place with a secure lock-up, Swan Eaton having nothing to boast about in that respect. The three who remained behind were left to the realization of their deliverance.

Anne got up from the stair on which she had sunk during the struggle. Miss Silver, coming into the hall, saw her half-way down, her hands in Jim's hands, her eyes seeing no one but him. She withdrew into the kitchen, but having assembled the meal, she returned to say briskly and firmly that lunch was ready and they had better have it. It was a quarter to two, and it was not to be supposed that any of them had made a good breakfast.

It was a strange meal. Anne had the feeling that she had died and come back to life again — a new life, a very happy life. She had her memory back, and after all this lonely time she had Jim. Everything settled into its place. She knew now the motive behind the attack upon her. She told Jim and Miss Silver what she now remembered.

"I got a letter just before Mavis was married. She was the friend I went round the world with, and she fell headlong in love and married an American. I would have stayed over there a little, but just before the wedding there was a letter from my solicitors, Thompson & Grant, to say that my old great-uncle William Forest had died, and had left all he had between me and my cousin Anne Forest Borrowdale. So you see, she was my cousin." She turned to Jim. "Poor Anne! Her father's mother was Anne Serena Forest, and she was a sister of old Mr William Forest. My father was his nephew, and Ross Cranston's father was another nephew. But Ross blotted his copybook rather badly and Great-Uncle William cut him out of everything. He left his fortune between Anne and me. I'd always known about it, but I don't think she had. Her father quarrelled with his relations over here. I don't know what it was all about now, and Anne didn't know. Her father never wrote to anyone or had any letters from England, she said. And I don't suppose Leonard Borrowdale ever thought about William Forest, or that there might be money coming to his daughter from him."

"He never said anything about it to me," said Jim.

"Well, there it is. I shall have to see the solicitors. There was quite a lot of money, I believe."

Miss Silver looked from one to the other. She said, "This Mr Cranston is a relation of yours?"

Anne flushed. She said, "Yes, he was the same relation to old William Forest that I was. He has never been —" She hesitated, and finished very low, "satisfactory. I'm afraid he thought that if he could marry me it would be all right — for him. I think they must have known that I would come to the Hood. I think when Anne turned up there that they must have felt desperate. I don't know what she said to them. If she said she was married, they would want to get her out of the way. You see, if she — wasn't there — everything came to me. I'm afraid that's what they thought of. So they made a plan — to kill her."

Tears were in her eyes. They ran down before she could stop them. Poor Anne — poor, poor Anne —

Miss Silver leaned forward and patted her hand.

"My dear," she said very kindly, "I do not think that you have anything to reproach yourself with." She rose to her feet. "Sit still and rest for a little. Inspector Abbott will be returning, and he will expect to find us ready to go back to town with him . . . No, I can manage very well, Mr Fancourt. I would rather that you kept Anne company. I do not think that she should be left alone just now."

Jim threw her a grateful glance. He insisted on carrying out the plates and dishes. Then he returned to Anne.

She had dried her eyes, and she was gazing out of the window at the dark trees which surrounded the house. He came to her and put his arms about her. They stood there together and looked out, not at the dark trees, but at the bright misty future. It was all

276

over, the trouble and the tragedy. They could not see their way clearly, but they would find it together. They stood there and faced it.

Also available in ISIS Large Print:

The Key

Patricia Wentworth

It's nearing the end of World War II, and Michael Harsch has been working for the government on a secret project for years. Finally, he is ready to hand over the precious formula for a groundbreaking new explosive — harschite.

But the next morning he is found dead, shot in the church where he used to go and play the organ. It looks like suicide, but Sir George Rendel believes otherwise. He knows that Harsch was due to deliver the formula — they'd made an appointment for later that day and Harsch was always very punctilious about his appointments. Sir George is determined to see the murderer caught.

But when the police nail the wrong man, there's nothing for it but to bring in Miss Silver . . . much to the chagrin of Chief Inspector Lamb.

ISBN 978-0-7531-8120-1 (hb)
ISBN 978-0-7531-8121-8 (pb)

Eternity Ring

Patricia Wentworth

Wentworth is a first-rate storyteller   **Daily Telegraph**

Patricia Wentworth has created a great detective in Miss Silver   **Paula Gosling**

Mary Stokes was walking through Dead Man's Copse one evening when she saw, in the beam of a torch, the corpse of a young woman dressed in a black coat, black gloves, no hat and an eternity ring set with diamonds in her ear. But when she and Detective Sergeant Frank Abbott went back to the wood, the body had vanished. This would have been mystery enough for Miss Silver . . . but then a woman reported that her lodger had gone out on Friday dressed in a black coat, black beret, black shoes and large hoop earrings set all around with little diamonds like those eternity rings. She never came back . . .

ISBN 978-0-7531-7656-6 (hb)
ISBN 978-0-7531-7657-3 (pb)

Out of the Past

Patricia Wentworth

James and Carmona Hardwick are spending the summer playing host to numerous friends and relatives in an old Hardwick family residence by the sea.

The arrival of Alan Field, a devastatingly handsome though shady figure from Carmona's past, destroys the holiday atmosphere in the ugly old house and replaces it with mounting tension, culminating in murder.

Fortunately for the Hardwicks and their guests, Miss Silver is present to unravel the secrets from the past — secrets the killer will stop at nothing to keep hidden.

ISBN 978-0-7531-7658-0 (hb)
ISBN 978-0-7531-7659-7 (pb)

The Case is Closed

Patricia Wentworth

The Everton murder case has long been closed. The culprit has been charged with the murder of his uncle and has served a year of his sentence already. Or has he?

The evidence against Geoffrey Grey is convincing but his wife believes in his innocence. And so does her young cousin, Hilary, who decides to solve the mystery herself.

But when Hilary is nearly murdered she turns in desperation to her ex-fiancé for help. Fortunately, he is acquainted with the singular Miss Silver, who is only too pleased to be asked to investigate.

ISBN 978-0-7531-7660-3 (hb)
ISBN 978-0-7531-7661-0 (pb)